zara

BY THE SAME AUTHOR

Historical fiction

At the Sign of the Sugared Plum
Petals in the Ashes

Contemporary fiction

Megan
Megan 2
Megan 3
Holly
Amy
Chelsea and Astra: Two Sides of the Story

zara

Mary Hooper

BLOOMSBURY

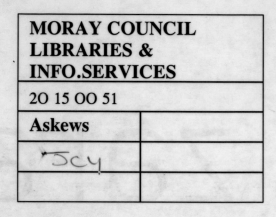
First published in Great Britain in 2005 by Bloomsbury Publishing Plc
38 Soho Square, London, W1D 3HB

Copyright © 2005 Mary Hooper
The moral right of the author has been asserted

A CIP catalogue record of this book is available from the British Library

ISBN 0 7475 7563 0

All papers used by Bloomsbury Publishing are natural, recyclable products
made from wood grown in well-managed forests. The manufacturing
processes conform to the environmental regulations of the country of origin.

Typeset by Dorchester Typesetting Group Ltd
Printed in Great Britain by Clays Ltd, St Ives plc

1 3 5 7 9 10 8 6 4 2

www.bloomsbury.com/maryhooper

www.maryhooper.co.uk

*For the library service,
and Yateley Library in
particular, who always
manage to find that
elusive book*

Chapter One

It started as a joke. At least, that's what I thought it was. Just Zara mucking about.

It was Friday and she and I were sitting at the back of class when she passed me a note. Nothing new there; we often spent the best part of our last period sending notes to each other. The thing was, this note wasn't in Zara's usual writing, all fancy with ballooning tops to the tall letters, but was written in a frail and spidery hand. The words were weird, too. They said: *I am from beyond the grave.*

'What?' I screwed up my face and turned to stare at her. Then I wrote underneath, *What are you on about?* and pushed the note back towards her.

Zara read what I'd written and just stared back at me, her eyes wide and startled. She had a stunned expression, as if she'd just seen something amazing and frightening. Or was trying to pretend she'd just seen something amazing and frightening.

I made the same sort of face back. If it was a joke, I was going to go along with it, although I had no idea what she was up to this time. I guess this was why I liked being mates with her. She was very slightly freaky – not enough to be alarming, just enough to be interestingly different.

The bell went, but as it was home time and we didn't have another class to go to we stayed in our seats. I gave her a nudge. 'What did you mean? Why did you write that?'

She paused. 'Ella,' she said finally, 'have you heard of automatic writing?'

I shook my head. 'Don't think so.'

'Well, it's where you're holding a pen in your hand and then something – someone – takes possession of you and you just write stuff down without knowing what you're doing.'

'Right!' I said. 'You mean like a ghost or someone writes it for you?' I made a ghostly moaning sound, just to show willing. I wasn't going to waste time on this joke, however, because all around us the rest of the class were collecting their things and charging out of the room, practically knocking Miss Stimpson down in their efforts to get out of school and begin the weekend. I began to collect up my stuff. 'Home time!' I said. 'Let's go.'

Zara put her hand on my arm. 'Really, Ella,' she said earnestly. 'That's just what happened. I was sitting here with my pen in my hand not thinking about anything in particular and all of a sudden it started writing on its own.'

'Oh, yeah!' I scoffed. I *so* didn't believe her. 'And my dog can dance the Highland Fling.'

'You haven't got a dog,' Zara said impatiently. 'No, honest! Cross my heart and hope to die.'

I groaned and sat down. 'Do it now, then, while I'm watching you. Pick up the pen and get possessed again.'

I tried to keep a straight face while Zara grasped the pen and then, her face set with concentration, closed her eyes and lifted her hand so that it hovered above the paper. While she did all this in slow robot mode I studied her face carefully to see if she was peeping or her lips were twitching. She looked different that day, actually, because she'd gone a bit Goth lately and, though we weren't supposed to put on make-up at school, had drawn black lines around her eyes and was wearing a trace of blue lipstick. She had a new ear piercing, too, but she definitely wasn't allowed to get away with having jewellery at school so all her piercings just showed as tiny pinpricks around her ear and in her nose. Her hair wasn't looking great – it was either greasy or very heavily gelled; I wasn't sure which.

Not a lot seemed to be happening on the automatic writing front. 'Just as I thought. It's not working!' I said after a moment, picking up my things again.

'Wait!' Zara's hand slumped on to the paper, then, with a jerk, began moving. I glanced at her face but her eyes were still closed. Slowly, the pen moved across the paper. It wrote *Beware*, and then stopped.

'*Beware*,' I read out. 'You've written *Beware*. As if you didn't know,' I added.

She opened her eyes, looked down at the paper and gasped.

'Is that going to be all?' I asked a bit sarcastically. 'Just the one word?'

'Looks like it,' she said. 'That's probably all the spirit wants to say.'

'So if it's quite finished, shall we go before we miss the bus?'

She nodded, stared at the paper for another

moment and then screwed it up and lobbed it into the bin.

Another mad Zara idea, I thought, as we ran for the bus. I didn't believe a word of it – she was always doing stuff like that. It had started shortly after we'd first come to this school, because it was only then that we'd all got interested in star signs and our horoscopes, and finding out the signs of boys we fancied and trying to work out if we were compatible with them or not. We did other stuff, too, like games to discover the initial of who we were going to marry, and Zara said she could read tea leaves to see your future. She didn't do this very often because she and I both hated tea, and if you wanted your future told it had to be from the dregs in a cup of tea made with real leaves – not a bag – that you'd made and drunk yourself.

Zara had also tried 'dowsing', which was what you did when you couldn't choose between two or three things. You held a crystal on a chain over, say, a colour or a DVD or whatever, to see if it signalled 'yes' by swinging backwards and forwards, or 'no' by going round and round.

We liked doing all this. Well, it was something else to think about apart from exams and tests and stuff. I never got quite as interested in it all as Zara, though. She got books from the library about it; books about developing your psychic powers and becoming aware of your spiritual potential, all that sort of thing, whereas I'm not really interested to that extent. I'm more into pop music and animals and stuff. And boys as well, of course (not that I'd had a lot of experience there). Sometimes I wondered if Zara and I were all that compatible; if we were *natural* best friends. We'd become so mainly because I'd been two weeks late starting at our new school, and so had she, and all the other girls seemed to have formed their friendships by then and had found mates to sit next to, so she and I had rather been thrown together. At the time I was just relieved to have someone, but later I'd begun to wonder what would have happened if I'd started at the proper time: would I have become best friends with one of the top cats? Would I have made it to the in-crowd?

That afternoon we only just caught the school bus and, because we were late, all the decent seats had been taken and we had to go right to the front, behind the driver. Lolling across the long back seat where they nearly always sat were four girls from our class: Sophie, Sky, Poppy and Lois. Sophie and Sky were best friends and more or less dominated every-thing – not in a nasty way, they weren't bullies, but because they were more together, confident, sophisti-cated and prettier than anyone else in the class. OK, looks aren't everything, we have that rammed down our throats often enough, but I've noticed that when you get dealt the prettiness card, you usually get other stuff along with it. Like, these two, and all the other really attractive girls I know, are nice, confi-dent, funny and likeable *as well* as being good-looking. How fair is that? If there had been boys at our school they'd all have fancied Sophie and Sky, or The Two, as we sometimes called them, and the rest of us wouldn't have got a look-in.

The Two had their hangers-on, of course – but then we were all their hangers-on really, and Poppy and Lois were only slightly down the pecking order as far as looks and personality were concerned. The Four usually went round together, sat in assembly with their arms linked, and had an invisible label saying *Most Popular* taped to their foreheads. They not only looked good, but when they were together they were like some sort of variety act. They hammed things up, joked and made people laugh. They were the sort of girls who exaggerated; when you listened to them everything was *amazing*, or *unbelievable* or *hilarious*. From where we were sitting in the front we could hear Sky's shrieks of laughter and Sophie saying, 'Honestly! It was just so completely *incredible*!'

'So what was that all about in class?' I asked Zara as we sat down, puffing slightly. 'That bit of writing.' I put on a quavery voice. '*A message from beyond the grave.*'

She hesitated. 'What did you think? Did you believe me?'

'Think I'm nuts?'

'What would you say if I told you that it was perfectly true?'

'I'd say you were barking.'

'But it *could* be true, couldn't it? I *could* get messages from the Other Side. Where the dead things are . . .'

'Yeah, right,' I said, grinning.

She was silent for a moment, then she said, 'I do really think I'm psychic, though.'

I shrugged. 'Yeah, maybe. And maybe not.'

'I *could* be. How would you know? D'you remember me telling you about when I was little, and I saw this man on the landing?'

I nodded. Ages ago we'd been talking about where

we used to live, and Zara had told me that she and her mum used to live in a flat at the top of a big old house. One day she'd seen a man on the landing standing in the shadows, and she'd screamed, and her mum had come out and the man had just completely disappeared. She'd heard later, though, that a man had once lived in their flat and been killed in a fight on that very spot.

'And there was something else,' she said. 'Something I've never told you.'

'What?'

'Well, once I was going by a railway station and I started crying and couldn't stop and I didn't know why,' she said earnestly. 'The next day I looked in the paper and there had been a rail crash at that station that very night and four people had been killed.'

'That was just a coincidence,' I said.

'OK, it might have been – but what if it wasn't? Say I really *was* psychic.'

'I'd still say you were barking.'

She slipped her arm through mine. 'Would you still be friends with me?'

'Dunno,' I said. 'Not if you were *too* weird.'

'But we like weird stuff!' she said immediately. 'We like reading our star signs and doing make-believe spells at Hallowe'en to find out who we're going to marry. And we like *Buffy* and you and I went to a fortune-teller at the fair once to try and find out our futures.'

'OK, then,' I said grudgingly. 'But all that's only mucking about, isn't it? Like, no one really believes that everything you read in your horoscope is going to come true.'

'But what if someone really *was* psychic?'

'What if they were?'

'They'd be in touch with the spirit world. Able to foretell the future and do all sorts of other things.'

I thought about this. 'I wouldn't believe them,' I said. 'And anyway, reading your stars and going to some gypsy is one thing, but you wouldn't *really* want to know about your future, would you, in case it was horrible. Suppose you found out you were going to die in an awful accident or end up in a wheelchair or something?'

There was a short silence. 'So you wouldn't want to be best friends with someone who was psychic?' Zara said eventually.

'No thanks!'

Zara didn't say anything for a moment. The bus was noisy, but over it all could be heard The Four, singing together in the back row. After a couple of moments one of them hit a bum note and they all started laughing. 'Oh well, I don't suppose I am really,' Zara said. After another moment she added, 'But Ella, I was thinking . . . it might be a laugh to pretend to be.'

I didn't reply straightaway because I was looking at Sophie and wondering why my hair wasn't all straight and silky like hers.

'I'm talking!' Zara said. 'Stop making sheep's eyes at them all the time!'

'What?' I turned back from looking at The Four. 'Sorry. Didn't realise I was.' I tried to put my mind to what she was saying. 'But why would we pretend to be psychic?'

'Just for fun. We could be special. Like those.' She jerked her thumb towards The Four. 'We could tell all the girls' fortunes and everyone would make a fuss of us and always want us around.'

I thought about it. Put like that, it sounded good. Who wouldn't want to be as popular as them? To be a girl the others looked up to, wanted to sit next to and whose name always popped up when it came to choosing names for anything. To be in demand all the time.

'We'd be special,' Zara said. 'You and I could do a double act.'

'What d'you mean? Do magic or something?'

'Not magic!' she said. 'Not getting rabbits out of hats. Look, I was reading this book by a magician – one of the modern sort of magicians. They call him psychic but he's not really. What he is, though, is he's very, very perceptive. He's alert to things like body language and eye movements, and sensitive to the things people don't say.'

'What's that supposed to mean?'

She looked at me earnestly. 'You have to listen between the lines.'

I frowned. 'I don't get it.'

She thought for a moment. 'Well, suppose I asked you how you did in your exams, and you replied that you had a job anyway, or that exams didn't really matter in the great scheme of things, then I'd take it from that that you'd bombed out and got all Es or something.'

I nodded. 'OK, I see. So if I asked you where you were going on holiday this year and you said you thought holidays were boring and a waste of time then I'd know you couldn't afford one.'

'Exactly. I mean – look at this automatic writing

business! I saw someone on the telly who said he'd had letters from all sorts of people: Elvis, Princess Di, Shakespeare and so on. People make a fortune out of it! And who's to say if they're genuine or not?'

'Search me,' I said.

When the bus reached my stop, Zara said goodbye and that she'd see me the next day, because we always went shopping on a Saturday morning. She added, 'And Ella, when you go to bed, think about me, and think about what I've said. I'm going to send you a special psychic message . . .'

'Right!' I said, and I rolled my eyes at her and grinned.

As I got off, I shouted goodbye down the bus. A few voices shouted back – enough to enable me to pretend, as I usually did, that The Four had noticed that I was getting off, had shouted their goodbyes and were now talking about me. 'Nice girl, that Ella,' they were saying. 'Yeah, I really like her.'

OK, I knew they weren't really, but it didn't do any harm, did it?

I walked home. I live in a newish, biggish house on the edge of an estate containing lots of similar houses – all quite boxy and ordinary. The best thing about ours, so Mum reckons, is that because it's a corner plot it has a really long garden that merges into woods and fields at the end.

There are four of us. My brother Toby is seven years older than me and in the last year of university. He's OK, but because of the big age gap between us, we'd never been particularly close, and he probably regarded me as a silly little kid and thought I was still playing with Barbies. It was a bit of a dead loss having that many years between us, because I knew I'd never be able to go round with him and his mates like girls did whose brothers were about the same age. Anyway, Toby's mates all seemed to be boffin types and I wouldn't have *dared* fancy any of them.

My dad works for a computer firm and my mum works as a manager in an old people's home. Both of them are fairly OK most of the time, although Dad has his moments: he's quite bossy and a bit of a snob, which means he's always criticising my friends and picking me up on how I pronounce words. He's got a thing at the moment about words ending in two 'l's – words like 'tell', 'well' and 'smell' – he says I pronounce them 'tewl' and 'wewl' and 'smewl' and he drives me absolutely mad repeating those words after me, properly, whenever I say them. Mum is much more easygoing and doesn't do stuff like that. She doesn't like any sort of an argument; anything for a quiet life, her motto is.

They're quite reasonable as families go; we do have rows but they aren't those stupendous ones that you hear about when everyone throws plates and stuff. Once I reached about thirteen I started getting on quite well with my mum, so much so that she even paid for the two of us to have a weekend away together at a health farm. I mean, I wouldn't go so far as to say my mum is my best friend or anything sloppy like that, and I certainly don't tell her about boys I fancy, but we do get on fairly OK.

That evening passed, as boring as usual: meal, bit of homework, TV, couple of CDs on headphones in my room, and then into bed. Just when I was on the point of falling asleep, though, I did one of those frightening starts that wake you up with your heart pounding away like mad. I felt – or thought I felt – someone breathing right close to me, and when I opened my eyes and looked into almost total darkness, I seemed to see Zara's face there in the air in front of me. I let out a stifled gasp, became fully awake and struggled into a sitting position, but as my eyes got accustomed to the dark I saw, of course, that there was nothing there. No Zara at all.

It was then that I remembered what she'd said about thinking about her as I went to sleep. Surely she hadn't somehow *spirited* herself to appear? No, of course not. That was ridiculous.

I slid back under my duvet and gradually my heart slowed down. It was OK, it had been nothing. I'd just somehow remembered Zara's words and had dreamt about her, that was all.

♉ Chapter Two

'Meeting Zara today?' Mum asked over breakfast the next morning.

I nodded.

'Does the Pope wear a long frock?' Dad said, putting down his bacon sandwich.

I shot him a look. He obviously thought he was being witty.

'Well, when *don't* you see her?' he went on. 'Haven't you got any other friends?'

'Of course I have,' I said. Though, actually, I thought to myself, have I?

'I *like* going round with her,' I said heatedly, even so. 'She's a laugh.'

'Hmm. I can see why the sight of her makes anyone laugh.'

'Don't be so horrible!'

Mum stuck an egg on toast in front of me. 'Don't

start anything,' she said to me. 'I've been looking forward to a nice quiet morning.'

'I haven't started anything!' I protested. 'That's so unfair! It's him. Tell him!'

'*Tell*,' Dad repeated, pronouncing the word like he was on the BBC or something. '*Tell* him. How many times do I have to say that before you improve?'

I groaned.

'I was just pointing out that it doesn't always do to live in another person's pocket,' he went on. 'And, let's be frank, sometimes I can't help wishing that you'd chosen someone else to be "best friends" with.' And he said the 'best friends' bit like it was the stupidest thing in the world to have a best friend.

'You're such a snob!' I said. 'Just because Zara's got a couple of piercings and she doesn't live in a very nice place –'

'Piercings! All round her ear and through her nose. God knows what else she's got with rings on.'

'She's got a couple of ear piercings and one tiny little stud in her nose and I think they look really good.'

'Really good?' he repeated witheringly. 'I don't think much of your taste.'

I slammed down my knife and fork, exasperated.

'Look, my friends are nothing to do with you! I don't tell you who you can –'

'*Tell* you,' he interrupted. 'There are two "l"s in the word.'

I could have screamed. 'You're friends with that idiot down the road who practically lives in the betting shop and –'

'Go to your room,' Dad snapped.

'I'm going!'

And to another sigh from Mum, I picked up my plate and went.

And so ended another happy family breakfast.

Dad, of course, was a bit of a control freak. I knew that all right, and thought I knew why: because he managed about twenty people at work and he liked to think he could manage me and Mum when he came home. He usually tried to bring Zara into things, saying that she was the wrong sort of friend to have and that by going round with her I was lowering myself.

The thing was, the bad thing was, I sometimes thought he was right. The piercings – well, he was always bringing those up. It was one of his big things: *pierced* equalled *common* in his book, and with each extra piercing your commonness increased. Zara, I knew, had had her ears pierced for the first time when she was just a baby, and by the time we were going round together had several piercings around the top curl of her ear. Last year she'd had a tiny little stone put into her nose and – worst sin of all and thank God Dad didn't know about it – she'd also had her belly-button pierced.

I thought all these looked cool, actually, and I was quite jealous of them. Because Dad had such a thing about ears being pierced I'd not been allowed to have mine done until my fourteenth birthday, and even then Dad had kicked up a stink and it had caused a row between him and Mum, because it had been her who'd taken me along to the hairdresser's to get them done. I'd been so thrilled, though, that afterwards I'd taken up a new hobby: earring-making, and spent hours in my room fiddling with bits of wire and threading tiny beads on minuscule chains. Everyone got earrings for their birthdays and Christmases from me, so much so that they were at saturation point with them and I'd started making little wire bracelets for a change.

I'd more or less forgotten about the row by the time I went off to meet Zara. Dad was a complete nightmare sometimes, but I figured that that was his problem, not mine. I tried not to let it get to me.

Zara was waiting for me on the wall that ran around the open space outside our shopping mall, wearing low-cut black jeans and a short T-shirt with a skull on it which showed off her belly-button piercing. Her hair was what she called 'interestingly messy', which meant she'd put masses of gel on it and then scrunch-dried it without a brush so that it now hung all over her face in knots and tangles. This wasn't a terrific look, to be honest, but at least she was different.

I sat down next to her, feeling drab. I was dressed much the same as I always dressed out of school: in jeans and a grey sweatshirt, with nothing in the way of gel on my hair or even much of a style to it. It could have been worse, I suppose, I could have been wearing a pink sweatshirt and my hair could have been tied back with ribbon instead of string, but looking as I did I felt a total frump compared to Zara.

We usually sat outside the mall for a while so we could talk about what we wanted to get, and plan what shops we were visiting and in what order. We didn't ever have much money to spend, but whether we had it or not didn't make much difference;

shopping still took up the best part of the day.

'OK?' she asked as I sat down.

I nodded, and it was only then that I remembered what had happened the previous night. 'Hey, listen to this . . . what did you say to me when I got off the school bus last night?'

She shrugged. 'Can't remember. See you tomorrow?'

'No. Something about sending me a psychic message.'

She stared at me, startled. 'Oh yes! What happened, then?'

'I kind of dreamt you; saw your face looming up in front of me. I tell you, it did my head in!'

She gasped. 'What did you actually *see*?'

'Well . . .' I struggled to remember but the memory had gone all fuzzy in the same sort of way that a dream does. 'It happened just as I was going to sleep . . .'

'What time?'

'Gone eleven. Eleven-thirtyish.'

She nodded eagerly. 'That's right. That's *just* when I was thinking of you.'

'I jumped – you know, did a big twitch. And then I opened my eyes and it was as if I could see your face projected in front of me.'

'Wow,' she breathed.

'What d'you mean – *Wow*?'

'Well, I told you I was psychic, didn't I? I was thinking of you; sending you a message just at that time – and you received it.'

I didn't know whether to burst out laughing or just rubbish her. 'Oh yeah!'

'That's called telepathy. It really works!'

I gave her a push and pointed at my foot. 'Try that. It's got bells on.'

'No, really, Ella!'

I shook my head and, though my expression was scornful, I must admit that a part of me was wondering if there was anything in it. 'It was just a dream,' I said.

She looked at me carefully, like she was assessing me, and then she said, 'So perhaps I just put the suggestion into your mind and it went into your subconscious and you remembered it just as you were falling asleep.'

I nodded. 'That's more like it.' It all made sense. More or less. I jumped up. 'Where to first, then? And where shall we eat?'

She stayed sitting on the wall. 'Did you think

about what I said, then? About pretending to be psychic and spooking everyone?'

I shrugged. I hadn't, up till then. But why not? It would be a laugh. 'Yeah. Yeah, let's do it!' I said.

'OK,' she said, smiling, pleased. 'We'll make the plans later.'

And we set off shopping, for once not having any particular notion of where we were going.

A couple of hours later, when we were sitting on the top floor where the food places were and eating pancakes, we looked over and saw Sky and Sophie on the floor below. They were leaning against the glass wall that ran right round the place and talking to a tall, good-looking guy with black, thickly-gelled hair.

'Get a load of him,' I said. 'Some girls get all the luck.'

'Some girls get all the looks,' Zara said.

'Too right.' Out of school uniform, Sky and Sophie looked even more stunning than usual. Best friends sometimes look alike, but Sky and Sophie weren't at all. Sky was small and shapely, with a smooth olive skin and dark spiky hair. She had blue eyes – a very bright blue – and had told us they were why she'd been called Sky. Her mum, apparently, had wanted to call her Heaven, but luckily her dad had put a stop to that. Sophie was taller than Sky (tall enough to be a model, which was where she was heading) with very long, very straight blond hair that fell in a waterfall down her back. As well as all this, though, they both had a kind of glow about them; a bonus extra that you couldn't quite fathom.

'Look at them,' Zara said a bit sourly. 'Bet you're thinking what I'm thinking. Don't they make you *sick*?'

That hadn't been what I'd been thinking at all, so I didn't reply.

Zara nudged me. 'They *do*, though, don't they? Bet you'd hate to be best friends with one of them!'

'I suppose so,' I said, though actually I was thinking, just give me half a chance. 'I bet they never have bad hair days,' I went on.

'Or spots!'

'Or snotty colds.'

We giggled and I carried on staring, as if I could somehow work out where all their assets came from and harvest some of them for myself. After a moment Sky suddenly looked up, saw us and waved. She nudged Sophie and I heard – or lip-read – her saying, 'There's Ella!' and Sophie waved as well. And then they said something to the guy and he grinned.

I think Zara must have realised that they hadn't mentioned her, because she suddenly said scornfully, 'Yes, well, we could all look like that if we had the money. But then again we don't all want to be footballers' wives, do we?'

I didn't say anything and we carried on eating our pancakes, with me taking the occasional look over the balcony, and a bit later Lois and Poppy came along and the four girls all greeted each other as if they'd been apart for six months. The fit guy was introduced and after a while went off on his own and they all stood staring after him, nudging each other and whispering. After that, two by two and arm in arm, they made their way into the big card shop nearby. From where we were sitting we could hear little giggles as they walked in. One of them was saying, 'He's *gorgeous*! How on earth did you manage to pull him!?' and one of the others was shrieking with laughter and saying she couldn't believe she *had*. From this distance, they all sounded the same and we couldn't tell whether it was Sky or Sophie who'd snaffled him. I was fascinated by all this – it was like watching one of the soaps, but in the end Zara got irritated and said for God's sake couldn't I stop looking, and anyway, was I with them or with her?

* * *

When we'd finished shopping we went back to Zara's house. We didn't usually go to hers, but it was closest and her mum had said that she'd be out until later that evening. Zara's bedroom, I noticed as soon as I went in, had gone Goth too. It now had a great big map showing the positions of all the signs of the zodiac, and there was purple muslin draped over the windows, and candles and crystals along the windowsill.

We began working out how we were going to do the horoscope scam. Well, I say *we* began working it out, but it was really all Zara's doing. She'd read loads of books about using your psychic abilities, 'developing your sensitivities', she called it, and had already worked out some tricks.

'What we've got to do first of all, very subtly, is let everyone know that I'm psychic,' she said. 'You can do that bit; tell them that I managed to find something you'd lost, or knew something was going to happen before it did. Everyone will be interested in that.'

'And then what?'

'Then we'll talk about horoscopes and stuff, and I'll say I can prove I'm psychic because I can work out what someone's star sign is without being told.'

'OK,' I nodded. 'But you might know people's star signs anyway. We all know when girls have had birthdays in the year and you could have remembered them.'

'Not if I don't know who I'm talking to . . .'

'What d'you mean?'

'Well, what if I'm blindfolded – or in a cupboard or something where I can't see anything – and one by one the girls come to stand in front of me and I can tell what sign they are just by sensing it.'

I blinked at her. 'How are you supposed to do that?'

'Because you and I will have worked out a code between us!'

I must have had a baffled expression on my face because she went on, 'Look, we'll find out the star signs of everyone in our class – that'll be easy – and then you'll memorise them. When we're doing the trick, you bring whoever it is to stand in front of me, then say something about beginning whenever I like.'

'*And?*' I screwed up my face, bewildered.

'And from what you say, I'll be able to tell what sign they are.'

'How?'

'Because we'll have a code which we'll have worked out between us! Like, say it's a girl who's Leo – when you lead her up you'll say a sentence beginning with L.' She thought for a moment. '"Look out, Zara. Here's a tough one." And Aries could be, "Are you ready for this one?"'

'OK,' I said slowly. I thought for a moment. 'But there are two Ls – Libra and Leo. And two Cs and two Ss.'

'Easy. So the second letter of the star sign will begin the next word in the sentence. Like, Libra starts L I so you could say, um . . . "Look into your mind and tell us what sign this girl is, Zara." Something like that.'

I sat and thought some more about it, and what a laugh it would be to be the centre of attention and be talked about by everyone, and what a change from the usual boring stuff we did at school. I'd only been noticed, really noticed, perhaps twice in my whole school life. Once had been at primary school when I'd fallen over in the playground, gashed my forehead open and had to be taken to hospital in an ambulance, and once a couple of years back when my brother had come in to give a talk about university life. He'd stayed on to eat in the school canteen with me at lunchtime and because we never got to see boys in our school, they'd practically mobbed him; gone mad for him.

Eventually I said to Zara, 'Wow! Do we really dare?'

'Course we dare,' she said. 'It'll be a laugh. And from that we can move on to other things.'

'What other things?'

'Tarot cards and stuff. And we can hold a seance.' She shivered excitedly. 'I've always wanted to go to a seance.'

I wasn't quite sure what this would involve – if it was anything to do with seeing ghosts I wasn't going to be keen on it – but I nodded just the same. 'We'll amaze everyone, won't we? Sky, Sophie . . . they'll all want to be friends with us.'

'No gathering will be complete without the famous twosome, Zara and Ella! We'll be sensational – just you wait!'

As I was staying at Zara's that evening we'd planned on eating together, but about six o'clock her mum came in unexpectedly.

Zara's mum. Well, I don't think my own mum is anything special, but next to hers mine is Supermum.

Hers, to be quite honest, is a bit of a horror. She's quite a big woman with lumpy white legs which, because she wears very short skirts, you usually see too much of. She wears lots of gold-coloured jewellery, including big hoop earrings practically down to her shoulders, and I always thought it was a good job we didn't live closer to them because if Dad was bothered about Zara then he'd have had a fit if he'd seen her mum. When Zara and I started going round together it was ages before I met her mum. We always met at mine and hung round at mine, and in the end I began to wonder if she had a parent at all. We eventually met up when Mum and I bumped into the two of them at the local supermarket. I was a bit shocked, seeing her for the first time, but I covered it up, of course. Afterwards Mum started to say something to me, something expressing surprise at her appearance, but I pretended not to know what she was on about. 'She looks all right to me,' I said, though actually she hadn't done at all.

The other thing was, she was a drinker. I knew that because her speech was often slurred and she was sometimes 'poorly' when I went round there. Besides, I'd seen her often enough coming out of the local offy with a bottle under her arm. On this particular day she said she had a headache, was going to bed and wanted no noise around the house.

Zara just sighed and rolled her eyes at me, so I thought it best to disappear. She gave me some homework: I had to try and learn the dates that all the star signs began and ended, ready for our debut at school the following week . . .

Chapter Three

'I'm glad there aren't more than twelve signs of the zodiac,' I muttered to Zara on the school bus. 'We'd never manage if there were.'

'Oh, we'd manage fine!' she said. Her eyes glittered. 'I can't wait to get going. It's exciting, eh, Ella?'

'Yeah, but what if it goes wrong, though?'

'It won't! Besides, even if we do get something a bit wrong, that'll be OK. Everyone makes mistakes – I bet even a real psychic does.'

'It's not getting their signs wrong as much as getting found out,' I said. 'Suppose they realise it's all a trick . . .'

'So what?' she said airily. 'We'll just say we were having a laugh.' She nudged me. 'Lighten up, girl! Go on, try out the codes again.'

And for about the twentieth time, we went

through our key phrases: the phrases we'd devised and which I would say as I led each girl to stand in front of a blindfolded Zara. These were:

ARIES	Are you ready, Zara?
TAURUS	Try and guess this one
GEMINI	Get ready for the next
CANCER	Can you do the next girl now?
LEO	Leading up the next girl now
VIRGO	Very good so far, now try this one
LIBRA	Look into your heart and tell us what this one is
SCORPIO	See how you get on with this one
SAGITTARIUS	Someone new is here now
CAPRICORN	Coming up with someone new now
AQUARIUS	Another girl's standing here now
PISCES	Please can you do this one

It had been impossible to work out the wording just as we'd wanted it to, but it was close enough. And as Zara said, if she got one wrong it would look more plausible. It wouldn't do to be absolutely perfect, she said.

Finding out the girls' zodiac signs had been easy. There were thirty-two girls in our class and we knew the signs of at least half without having to look them up. The birth dates of the others – those who didn't join in the reading of newspaper or magazine predictions – we found on our class register and I'd jotted their signs down and tried to learn them off by heart. We didn't reckon on having thirty-two girls all in at once, anyhow – or anywhere near that number. Some girls just weren't interested in that sort of thing.

It was dead easy getting the subject introduced. What we did was start talking about psychic stuff at our table at lunchtime and then, in a dramatic voice such as one of The Four would use, I said that Zara was probably a witch; that she was just *amazing* at predicting things.

'She's always telling me weird stuff,' I said. '*And* she's seen a ghost.'

Some of the others had already heard about the man in the flat incident. Now Lois, really interested, wanted to know what else Zara could do.

'Well, I don't really know because I've only just

started developing my psychic side,' Zara said earnestly. 'Up till now I've been pushing it into the background and pretending it doesn't exist.'

'Why would you want to do that?' Sky said. 'It would be *amazing* to be psychic.'

'It can be pretty scary, though,' Zara said, and she told them about when she'd gone past the train station and started crying, and how she'd found out about the accident in the papers the following day.

As I listened to her I suddenly felt uneasy. This was obviously something that had actually happened . . . Did this mean Zara really *was* psychic? And in that case, was she just pretending to me that she wasn't in case it scared me off?

'I felt bad about it afterwards, wondering if I could have done anything to save the people on the train,' Zara finished with a sigh. 'And I've never forgotten about it.'

'It was probably all just a coincidence,' Sophie said – she had just squashed herself down on the end of the table next to Sky. 'Because mostly it's just a lot of rubbish. I know we read our horoscopes, but we don't really believe all those things are going to come true, do we?'

There were several voices of protest, some of the girls saying that they'd met someone special or come into a sum of money exactly when their horoscope had said they would.

'More coincidences!' Sophie said, shaking back her hair so that it rippled across her back. 'How can someone predict what's going to happen to one twelfth of the population?'

'They can predict a trend,' I said, because I'd been reading up about that sort of stuff myself. 'Like, if two warring planets are coming up against each other in your chart it might signal that you're going to have a row with someone.'

'Huh!' Sophie scoffed, and a couple of the others looked as if they agreed with her.

'But being psychic can mean lots of different things. In the olden days people who could see into the future were called *sensitives*,' Zara said. 'It just meant they were finely tuned into the feelings of other people, and sometimes those other people were alive and sometimes they were dead. I like to think that's what I am – a sensitive.'

A couple of the girls started laughing, then, and Zara protested. 'You can laugh! I am, though.'

'She is. She gets feelings about things,' I said

earnestly. 'And I know it's true about that train crash.'

'OK! Prove you're psychic, then,' Sophie said bluntly.

Zara smiled. This was just what she'd wanted. 'What d'you want me to do?' she said to Sophie and the small crowd which had gathered round our table.

'Tell me what's going to happen to me and when I'm going to meet the love of my life,' someone said.

'Yeah, I want to know that, too,' said Sky.

Zara shook her head. 'I can't predict big, important stuff like that for all of you. For one thing there's not enough time, and for another it would be really tiring. You'd have to have a one-to-one personal reading for that.'

'Do something about star signs, then,' I said, because although we'd agreed that it would look better if the suggestion didn't come from me, there didn't seem to be any other way of bringing it up. 'Why don't you try and sense what everyone's star sign is?'

'Yeah, that's a good one,' Poppy said.

'But you know most of our signs already,' Sophie objected.

'OK, I know!' I said to Zara, as if it had just occurred to me. 'We'll blindfold you, and then I'll lead the girls up one by one and you've got to say what their star signs are.'

Zara put her hands to each side of her temple (so it looked as if she was communing with the spirits, she told me later) and closed her eyes briefly. Then she opened them and said she thought that was possible, and she would try to do it. 'We'll need to go somewhere quiet, though,' she said, looking round the teeming dining hall. 'And I can't promise it'll work, but I'll do my best . . .'

Eleven of us went off in the end. Our own tutor room was empty and though we weren't really allowed in there at lunchtimes, that's where we went.

I took a quick look round at the girls who were coming with us, feeling excited. I knew the phrases we were going to use off by heart, and already knew the star signs of about seven of the girls. The other four I'd have to look up, but I'd written down everyone's signs in a code on the back of my timetable, and I took a quick look at this whilst pretending to see what lesson we had next period. Someone went off to their locker to get the scarf which was to be tied around Zara's eyes, then she sat on a chair out at the front and everyone gestured quietly among themselves as to what order they were going to go forward.

I didn't have anything to do with the choosing, but just led each girl down in turn and let Zara know by our prearranged phrase that someone was there in front of her. I was nervous at first, but the words I had to say sounded completely natural with a laugh here and there, a hesitation or a few words tagged on at the end.

There was a lot of giggling from the girls at first, and some scoffing, but after about three girls had been up to stand in front of Zara and she'd got their signs right, everyone fell silent and the mickey-taking stopped. Zara got quite bold then and started adding little bits of information along with the star sign. When Poppy went up she said, 'Virgo. And someone who loves to write lists.' Which was perfectly true of Poppy. Of Sky she said, 'Sagittarius. And here's someone who loves enjoying herself and is always out and about.'

Sophie, unfortunately, was the only one that she got wrong. Or I got wrong, actually, because Sophie was Capricorn, and by mistake I gave the other 'C' phrase, for Cancer.

'No!' Sophie said triumphantly, when Zara said she was the sign of the crab.

Zara put her hands to each side of her head again. 'Ah. I got it wrong because this person is putting up barriers,' she said after a moment. 'She's blocking me out.'

Sophie grinned round at everyone, nodding agreement.

'This is a girl with secrets to hide,' Zara went on. 'And one big secret in particular.'

To my surprise, Sophie's smile dropped and a tiny twitch came at the side of her mouth. 'Rubbish,' she said. 'It's me – Sophie. And you've got me completely wrong!'

'Have I?' was all Zara said, quietly and meaningfully. 'Have you no secrets at all?'

Sophie didn't say any more, just sat down. The next girl waiting to go up was India; she was Pisces for sure.

I led her up to stand in front of Zara. 'Please can you do this girl next. Maybe you'll have better luck with her . . .'

'How was *that*, then?' Zara said as we closed my bedroom door behind us that evening. 'Wasn't it brilliant? They fell for it every inch of the way!'

I nodded. 'And even when I got Sophie wrong it

didn't really matter, because you turned it to your advantage by saying she was blocking you out.'

'Which she was.'

'But how did you know those other things,' I asked curiously, 'about Poppy liking to write lists and all that?'

'I'm psychic!'

'No, don't mess about. How did you know *really*?'

Zara shrugged. 'It's just typical behaviour for that star sign. Virgos like things neat and just-so – list-making is one of the things they do. And Libras spend so much time weighing things up that they can't make decisions.'

'What about Sophie, then? You said she'd got a secret.'

'Everyone's got secrets,' Zara said. 'Everyone's got something they don't want anyone else to find out.'

'She went all tight-lipped and twitchy when you said that.'

'I'm not surprised,' Zara said. 'She's got a really *big* secret.'

But when I asked how she knew this and what it was, she just laughed and said the spirits hadn't revealed that so far. And then she wouldn't say anything else about it.

We made plans to follow things up by doing something else psychic the following week. Everyone was going to put something small of theirs – a ring or a watch or whatever – into a covered box, and Zara was going to pull these things out one by one, hold it in her hand and then say something about its owner or its history. The proper name for this, she said, was 'psychometry'.

'Where do I come in?' I asked, not wanting to be left out. If Zara became really popular and in demand, then I wanted to be part of it.

'Well, you're my psychic assistant,' Zara said. 'I'll say I can only work with you because you give out the right sort of vibes.'

'But when you take objects out of the box, how will I tell you who owns what?'

'Just with your eyes,' she said. 'All you've got to do is watch what everyone puts in and then, when I pull it out, signal who it belongs to by glancing at them. Easy!'

'It sounds a bit hit and miss,' I said doubtfully. 'Aren't we going to have a code to back things up?'

'No need!' Zara said.

We talked a bit more about this and when it was time for her to go home I went downstairs to see her out. Unfortunately, Dad was just coming in.

'Not you here again!' he said to Zara. He was making out it was a joke, but I knew he really meant it.

Zara pretended to smile. 'Afraid so!'

'Had any new holes put in your body lately?'

'No, but ask me same time next week,' Zara said flippantly.

Dad looked at her, shaking his head. I knew he was going to come out with something awful but had no way of stopping him. 'How sad,' he said. 'Let's hope you grow out of it before you're completely riddled with cavities.'

She glowered at him. She's quite good at glowering if she doesn't like someone. 'None of your business,' she said and walked straight past him.

I was embarrassed for both of them. 'Sorry about him,' I muttered as I opened the gate for her. 'He thinks he's being funny.'

She shrugged. 'Dads, eh?' she said, and then added, 'Not that I've ever had one.' Her eyes gave a sudden gleam. 'You know I said something about everyone having secrets?'

'Yeah.'

'Well, your dad's got one.' She gave a shudder.

'And I don't think it's a very nice one. Bye!'

And before I could ask what she was on about, she walked off.

Chapter Four

'What did you mean?' I asked Zara as soon as I got on the school bus the following day.

'What did I mean about what?'

'You know – about my dad. About him having a secret.'

She turned in her seat to look at me. 'It's just . . .' And then she hesitated and her face became closed and guarded. 'No. It's probably nothing.'

'But you said he had a secret and it wasn't very nice.'

She was looking out of the window now, and wouldn't turn her head to look at me. I could see by the way her face was set that she wasn't going to say anything else. She often did this: started saying something, then changed her mind and clammed up.

I'd hardly slept the night before, just lain there tossing and turning and imagining all sorts of things about my dad. What was this secret? It could be one of a number of things and they all went through my head one by one. He was having an affair. He was a bigamist and had another family. He was leaving Mum. They were getting divorced. He'd lost his job. He'd done something bad – a robbery/drugs deal/hit-and-run and was being put in jail.

It was a horrible feeling. OK, I knew he was a bit of a pillock sometimes, but that didn't mean I wanted him out of my life. I'd got used to my dad. Annoying as he sometimes was, I couldn't imagine life without him.

About two o'clock in the morning, utterly fed up at being awake, I'd thought I'd try the automatic writing business. I got up, went over to my desk and pulled out a pen and a sheet of paper. Then I sat there with the pen hovering over the paper and my eyes closed, thinking, *Tell me what my dad's secret is . . .*

But it hadn't worked; the pen hadn't made as much as a mark on the paper. In the end I'd gone back to bed and eventually fallen asleep.

'I tried that automatic writing,' I said to Zara as our bus swung through the school gates. 'I wanted to know my dad's secret.'

'And what happened?' Zara asked, turning to me, suddenly interested.

'Nothing.' I shrugged. 'It didn't move.'

'That's because you're not psychic.'

'But nor are you, are you? You're not *really*.'

'Well, what do you think?' she asked. But while I was working out what to say the bus pulled up at the stop, there was a big rush to get off and I never did say anything. I didn't know, was the answer. I didn't know if she was really psychic or not.

That week we realised it was working – the popularity thing. At break different girls would wander over to talk to us, and at lunchtime would look to see where we were and come to sit on our table. Sky and Sophie and Poppy and Lois came too, and it might sound batty but it was strangely thrilling to have The Four actually seeking us out and wanting to sit with us. Sophie, actually, was the only one who was a little reluctant; not so interested in us as the others. She was the one who'd ask if we could *please* talk about something else and said it was boring hearing about star signs and creepy stuff the whole time. She preferred talking about soaps and bands and fashions.

As we were talking, Zara would every so often throw a little crumb into the general conversation, ask someone how their parrot was ('How did you know I had a parrot?' they'd say in awe) or tell them where they were planning to go on holiday next year ('How did you know that? My dad's only just booked it!').

Afterwards I would ask Zara how she knew this sort of stuff and she'd say it was because she actually listened to things, had heard Chloe talking about taking her parrot to the vet a couple of weeks back, or remembered Danielle mentioning ages ago that her family were looking at holiday brochures for the Caribbean. 'It's just being open to things: listening between the lines. Remember what I said at the start?'

I thought about this. 'What about my dad, though?' I asked. 'What could you have found out about him from listening to stuff?'

'That's different.'

'You said it was probably nothing . . .'

She sighed.

'Tell me what it is – what you *think* it is,' I said, for she was about to turn away again.

'Look, the honest answer is, I don't know,' she

said. 'I just got this weird feeling about him the other evening.'

For some reason I felt my mouth begin to go dry. 'D'you think it's something very bad?'

She shrugged. 'Dunno.' She looked at me. 'Nah, it's probably nothing. Forget it.'

As if.

On Thursday we were told that the following afternoon we'd be having an extended lunch hour because the teachers had a meeting, so that was the day we decided to do the psychometry thing. We told certain girls (it felt odd to be the ones doing the choosing – selecting and rejecting) to bring in a piece of jewellery or something small; something that Zara wouldn't recognise.

'It's got to be something of your own, though,' I explained in my role as psychic's assistant. 'If it belongs to someone else then the vibes will be wrong and Zara will get confused.'

I didn't ask anyone what they were going to bring, but Sophie came up to me and whispered that she was going to bring a silver bangle she'd been given when she was christened. She'd never actually worn it, she said, did I think that would be all right?

Surprised at being asked, because she'd said all along that she didn't really believe in it, I told her that that sounded fine. Chloe, too, came up and said she was bringing a signet ring which had been given to her by her brother; would it matter that she hadn't bought it herself? I assured her it wouldn't.

Going home on the bus that day, Zara asked me if I knew what any of the girls were bringing and, though I felt a bit uncomfortable about doing so, I told her about Sophie's silver bangle and Chloe's ring. It was silly to feel guilty, I said to myself, when the whole thing was a trick anyway. Zara seemed pleased with the information, especially when I said that Chloe's ring had belonged to her brother, but I didn't think any more about this at the time.

'Did you find out what Poppy's putting in?' she went on. 'I saw you chatting away to her.'

'No,' I said. 'We were just talking.'

'About me, was it? I could see her looking over, and then you both started laughing.'

'I can't remember what we were talking about,' I said. I felt my face turn red because I could remember exactly. Poppy and I had been laughing because she'd said that she wasn't surprised at what Zara was doing because she'd always thought she was a bit of a gypsy. 'Expect she'll be selling us lucky white heather next,' she'd whispered, and before I could stop myself I'd giggled and added, 'I wouldn't be surprised – you should see the state of her mum!'

I'd felt awful after. It was just one of those things that you come out with for the sake of being funny, though, and to carry on the conversation.

There were eight of us in our tutor room the following lunchtime: me and Zara, The Four, plus India and Chloe. I was intending to put something in the box too, as further proof of Zara's psychic powers.

Lois was late coming in and while we were waiting for her – with Zara sitting quietly meditating, head bowed and eyes closed – everyone else was talking about Sky's boyfriend. This, apparently, was the boy we'd seen them chatting to in the shopping mall a few weeks before. He was a DJ, and French, and wanted Sky to go to Paris with him for the weekend. They were discussing what she should tell her mum and dad, and whether they would let her go or not.

I thought I wouldn't have minded having her dilemma. Imagine having a proper boyfriend, some-one really fit, let alone one who was French, a DJ, *and* who invited you to Paris. I'd been to a funfair once with a boy, and met another on holiday who'd taken me to the cinema, but that had been about as exciting as it had got. We didn't exactly see a lot of boys. There was a boys' school just down the road from ours, but the ones in our year were unbelievably childish and we usually saw them rolling around the ground having play-fights. Perversely, the boys in the year above that, the ones we fancied, didn't sniff in our direction. At least, what I mean is, they didn't sniff in *mine*.

Listening to everyone talk that lunchtime, I thought that it was true what Zara had said about picking stuff up by just listening. People dropped all sorts of things into conversations when they were talking trivia; gave away lots of information about themselves. I knew that Zara, whilst pretending to be meditating, would be listening hard to all the chat going on.

'Just tell them you're going away with us!' Poppy said finally to Sky. 'We'll cover for you, won't we girls?'

India nodded. 'Course we will!'

Sophie didn't agree, though. 'Not that I wouldn't cover for you, Sky,' she said, 'but I don't think you should lie to your mum about something so big.'

'But I know she won't let me go if I tell the truth!' Sky said, her blue eyes clouding over.

'Well, there'll be other times,' Sophie said. 'If you don't go with him this time he's sure to ask you again.'

'But he wants me to go *now*!' Sky wailed.

At this point Lois came in. She was late, apparently, because she'd forgotten her object and had had to go home for it.

'OK, shall we start?' Zara said. 'Could you go round with the bell, please, Ella?'

This was a new refinement which I'd read about in one of Zara's books, and which gave me something important to do. I'd read that if you were going to do any psychic task in a room, then first you had to cleanse it of stale air and any harmful influences by going around its perimeter ringing a bell. Luckily, Zara already owned a Tibetan bell which she said made the right sort of noise, so I went to each corner of the room in turn and shook it. It all sounded a bit potty and I think I might have started giggling if anyone else had, but no one even smirked; they all just looked serious and expectant.

When I'd finished the cleansing ritual, Zara looked the other way and we all put our chosen objects in a box.

'Bet you've already told Zara what you're putting in!' Sophie said to me in an undertone.

I shook my head. 'I haven't. Honestly!' I said, and I was speaking the truth – even though I knew Zara would recognise the sparkly purse I was putting in because it had been her who'd given it to me.

I watched as everyone else put their things in. Chloe put in the signet ring, Lois a framed photograph, Poppy a key, India a watch she didn't usually wear and Sky a charm bracelet. Sophie put her object in last, but to my surprise it wasn't a silver bangle, but a cross and chain.

'Oh, you changed your mind,' I said.

She looked at me and raised her eyebrows. 'So I have. Is that OK, or will it present difficulties?'

I looked away, my face flaming. She'd guessed! She'd guessed I would have told Zara about any objects I'd found out about.

'Is that OK?' she asked again.

'Course it is,' I said carelessly, calming down a little. The fact that she'd put in something different didn't really matter: Zara would see that there wasn't a child's silver bangle there, and when Sophie's cross and chain came out I could signal to her who'd put it in anyway.

Zara pulled out the first object, which was India's watch. I was all ready to signal with my eyes who it belonged to, but Zara, cleverly, didn't even glance at me, just held the watch clasped in her hands with her head lowered, as if thinking deeply.

We were all silent. The class door was shut and outside it you could hear the life of the school going on, but here we were in our own closed little world. So far, I thought, it was all going brilliantly. Everything Zara and I had planned had worked. We had The Four here with us, eager for information, and even if Sophie suspected something there was no way she was going to find out the truth.

Zara lifted her head and, breathing in deeply, looked round the room. I quickly flashed my eyes towards India.

'This watch belongs to someone with a bubbly personality,' Zara began slowly. 'Someone who loves animals and who would speak out strongly if she ever felt one was being mistreated. Here is someone who loves the simple things in life, but also enjoys going out and about and having fun.' She looked round at us. 'Don't tell me yet whose it is, but am I right about her character?'

Someone – Poppy, I think – said yes.

'This person probably owns an animal or two. Maybe more!' Zara said, and there was an affirmative murmur from India, whose family had a handful of dogs. 'She comes from a friendly, rough-and-tumble sort of home and is one very happy girl.'

'What about this person's love life?' India asked.

Zara smiled. 'I think that she's already been madly in love once in her life,' she said, 'but has yet to meet that special person. In the meantime she's going to enjoy playing the field.'

India beamed, well pleased with this, but didn't say anything about it being her object. Zara put the watch down on the table and pulled out the next thing, which was Poppy's key. She hesitated for a moment, as if considering what she held, and then – without even glancing at me – began speaking.

Cleverly, all the things she said at the start, before she'd looked at me, were just general sorts of things. She said that the owner of the key loved dancing, sitting in the sun, shopping and going out – and of course, all those could have applied to any one of us. And when she looked round the group and I signalled to her whose key it was, *then* she added all the personal stuff, a few little extra things to make everyone's jaw drop at the accuracy of what she was saying.

Three more objects were brought out after Poppy's: mine and Sky's – these were quite straight-forward – and then came Chloe's ring. Zara already knew who this belonged to, of course, so didn't even glance at me. She started off by saying that the ring was owned by someone very sentimental and romantic. Someone caring, thoughtful . . . a nice girl.

No one said anything but the others were grinning, because she'd described Chloe exactly.

'This girl likes sports, she's dead keen on football and *mad* on one particular player in the England team,' she went on, and of course these things were true as well, because she knew full well the ring belonged to Chloe. She rolled the ring round and round in her fingers, 'The other important thing about this ring, though, is that the person who gave it to its present owner is, sadly, not with us.'

Listening to Zara, I thought she must have forgotten that I'd told her that it had been given to Chloe by her brother, and was guessing that a granddad or someone who'd died had given it. Chloe didn't say anything about this, though, just held out her hand for the ring.

'Spot on,' she said, and she put it back in her pocket.

I forgot about it then because the framed photograph came out next and I flicked my eyes towards Lois.

'This is someone's mother and she's in the spirit world,' Zara said solemnly, after holding the frame for just a moment. There was a muffled gasp from a couple of the girls, although actually we all knew that Lois's mum had died a while back, and this was obviously a photograph of someone's mother, so Zara only had to put two and two together. But it was *that* that she was so good at. She could put two and two together and make six.

'This is a photograph of someone who passed away nearly three years ago,' she added, 'and it may be that the anniversary of this death is quite close.'

The next few things she said . . . well, they startled Lois and they startled me as well.

'The person who owns this usually has it in full view,' Zara went on quietly. 'Her mum's favourite flower was anemones and there's a small bunch of artificial ones in a blue vase kept right next to it.'

Lois started and gave a little cry which Zara didn't appear to hear. She went on, 'Whoever of you it is, is looking after her mum's cat, even though she's allergic to its fur.'

Lois now gave the game away completely. 'Yes, I am!' she said. 'How could you possibly have known that?' She looked round at everyone and her eyes were bright with tears. 'My mum loved her old cat,' she said. 'He misses her nearly as much as I do.'

I think everyone was a bit awestruck and choked at this, and no one spoke for a while.

'D'you think you'd be able to contact my mum for me, Zara?' Lois suddenly burst out. 'Would I be able to speak to her?'

'I'm not sure,' Zara said. 'Maybe. Another time.'

A shiver went right down my spine. We were getting into something else now. Something I didn't much like the sound of.

No one spoke for a couple of moments, then Sophie said, 'The bell's going to go soon. Shall we have the last object?' Her cross and chain was the only thing which hadn't yet come out.

'OK,' Zara said, and she reached into the box and took it out, swinging the cross gently between her fingers for a moment or two. 'This object,' she said, 'doesn't belong to a member of this group. Someone's put in something that is not owned by them.'

No one said a word.

'And the reason they've done this is because they're scared I'll hold their object and find out something that I shouldn't.' Zara paused, 'Especially that big secret of theirs!'

There was a moment's silence, then Sophie gave a laugh. A funny, forced sort of laugh. 'OK, I own up!' she said, flicking her hair out of her face. 'It's my sister's cross and chain. I just thought I'd see if I could catch you out.'

'You'll have to try harder than that!' Zara said.

Sophie reached for the cross and chain.

'Hang on,' Zara said, holding it just out of her reach, 'Your sister was given this when she was a bridesmaid. She usually keeps it hanging over the mirror in her room.'

Sophie smiled. 'Good try, but not right,' she said, and then the bell went, everyone took their objects back and we went to sit in our own seats.

I felt vaguely uneasy. Why was Zara being odd with Sophie, so difficult, when the whole object of the game was to try and be popular and become special friends with her and Sky?

Something was wrong, but I didn't know what. As we sat down, though, Zara was smiling. She said to me in a whisper, 'Sophie's lying. Just you wait and see.'

♌
Chapter Five

The following Saturday Zara and I were shopping, as usual.

In one of the little roads on the old side of town, away from the shopping mall, Zara had discovered a shop called Dreaming which sold all sorts of spooky stuff like crystals and healing herbs, coloured candles, dream-catcher nets and Tarot cards. Going into this shop was like entering a grotto: cobwebby stuff was hanging from the ceiling and there were weird pictures on the walls, while little statues of gnomes and mystic indoor water-features stood on the shelves. I thought it was a bit creepy but Zara loved it; she kept saying she wanted to turn her bedroom into a miniature version of it.

We looked around in there for ages and she bought a couple of crystals which she said had spoken to her and asked to be bought. What she really, really wanted was a crystal ball, like witches have, but they were huge and cost nearly a hundred pounds. When she spoke to the man behind the counter, though, who was a real hippy, he told her that if she was psychic she didn't need a crystal ball but could *scry* in a bowl of clean water.

'What's *scry*?' I asked.

'Seeing pictures,' Zara said. 'Like when you stare into the fire and see pictures in the flames, or shapes in the clouds.'

She persuaded me to buy a crystal. I didn't actually want a crystal, would rather have put the money towards a new CD, but she said I must have a crystal and that it would protect me. She was so persuasive that I let her talk me into it, and then we spent about half an hour choosing the right one, getting them all out of their little straw baskets and holding them up to the light. I liked the look of a turquoise stone but she said a striped one called tiger's eye would be better and suit my personality more. I paid for it and the hippy man told me I had to wash it in running water frequently and, if it was around any particularly negative influences, I should also sprinkle it with salt, pass it over the smoke of an incense stick and then put it into the flame of a silver candle. These, he said, stood for the four elements: water, earth, air and fire. I wanted to giggle when he told us all this, but Zara was looking very serious so I didn't dare.

From Dreaming we went into the mall and did a quick round of our usual shops. I still liked all the accessories shops with their sparkly hair grips and bungees with ribbons and flowers on, but Zara didn't seem as interested in these as usual. She did ask me to make her a pair of earrings, though, and wanted them to be long, thin silver chains with black star-shapes on the end, so we spent some time in the bead shop.

After this we were starving and went upstairs for something to eat, and it was only here that we got some quiet time to talk about the psychometry business. There were loads of things I wanted to ask her.

'About that cross and chain,' I said, once we were sitting down with our fishcakes and chips. 'How did you know that it was Sophie's?'

'How did I know it *wasn't* hers, you mean?'

I nodded. 'That as well.'

'That was easy!' she said scornfully. 'Everyone's object had come out of the box by then and I hadn't found a child's bangle, so I knew whatever was next must be Sophie's. It was just a process of elimination.'

'OK. But then you said straightaway that it wasn't hers.'

'Well, that's because anyone can tell that Sophie isn't the sort of person to own a silver cross and chain,' she said. 'And besides . . .' her voice began to go all faraway, '. . . as I held it up I got a picture in my head. I saw it hanging over a mirror, and a girl looking at it who looked like Sophie but wasn't; someone who was younger. And then I knew it really belonged to her sister and not her.'

'But she said it didn't hang over a mirror.'

'I told you she's a liar,' Zara said bluntly.

I thought about this for a moment. 'So if you know this for definite, you really *are* psychic, then?'

She looked at me closely. 'Maybe I am. Maybe I'm not. What d'you think?'

I shrugged. 'I dunno. I mean . . . that automatic writing business you did – was *that* true?'

'No!' She shook her head, grinning. 'Got you going though, didn't it?'

'And you needed my help with the astrology game.'

'Only a bit. I could probably have done it on my own . . .'

I was confused. I stared over the balcony down to where we'd seen The Four just a few weeks before. It was only October and still warm out, but Christmas decorations were already being strung along the walkways.

'But you knew about those other things – about India's dogs, for instance,' I said.

'Oh, everyone knows she's got three dogs! I've even seen her dad waiting outside school with them. Things like that are simple to work out.'

'So what about Lois's mum and that vase of flowers?'

'I guessed.'

'Guessed the type of flower she had there? And the *colour* of the vase?!'

'I know! Clever, eh? I just . . . dunno . . . seemed to see them in front of me clear as day.'

'So you *are*, then. You really are psychic.'

She shrugged. 'Or maybe I'm just sensitive.'

'Didn't you say that was the same thing?'

She raised her eyebrows. 'Who knows. I'm whatever you want to think I am.' She grinned at me. 'It's great, though, isn't it? We've got them gagging for us. Everyone wants to be friends with us now.'

'I guess,' I said thoughtfully.

'And I'm going to do a Tarot reading and then we'll have a proper seance with a ouija board and everything.'

'What's that?'

'It's where you sit round in a circle and have all the letters of the alphabet on a table in the middle, and then you put your fingers on a glass and –'

'Oh yeah, I've seen it on a film,' I said. I'd seen it and hadn't much liked what I'd seen, because it had ended with a ghost being unleashed which they hadn't been able to get rid of ever again.

'You have to ask, "*Is there anyone there . . .*"' Zara said, lowering her voice to a hoarse whisper, 'and then a spirit enters into the glass and answers all your questions. And sometimes . . . sometimes you get someone coming through that you actually knew. Like if your uncle or dad had died they might come across with a special message for you. "Don't catch the train tomorrow because it's going to crash!" or something.'

I shivered. I've never been a great one for ghost stories or spooky films. It's not that I don't like being scared – I can watch quite gory stuff without turning a hair – it's just that anything about ghosts gives me the creeps. I even find *Buffy* a bit too much sometimes. I mean, if it was a choice between a week in the lions' cage at the zoo, or a night in a haunted house, I'd take my chances with the lions any time.

'I wonder if I've got a spirit guide,' Zara said.

'What's that?'

'A guide that comes through from the Other Side. The land where the dead dwell . . .'

'Oh,' I said, thinking that I didn't much like the sound of this.

'A guide acts as a medium and brings people's dead relatives to talk to them. Sometimes it's a Native American – you know, a Red Indian.'

I shivered. It was all getting a bit too weird for me. 'I thought we were just going to play a couple of games, get the other girls going a bit and get them interested. I thought it was just to make us popular! I didn't know you'd be calling on Native Americans and contacting the dead.'

'Yeah, but as it's going so well it seems a shame to stop now. And, besides, I've kind of started opening myself up . . .'

'What's that mean?'

'Well, I told you I always thought I *could* be psychic, but I'd never done anything about it. And then when I read those books about developing that side of you, letting it all out, I started to think more about those sorts of things and it all started to happen.'

A ghost caught my eye. A sparkly white ghost shimmering in the window of the shop below advertising stuff for Hallowe'en. It was hanging on a wire, moving up and down catching the light.

'But can't you stop being psychic now?' I asked Zara after a moment. 'Suppose you don't want to know anything else – can't you just stop?'

'I don't want to!' she said. 'And anyway, I don't think I can. They say in one book that giving your psychic power free rein is like turning on a tap and then losing the bit at the top. Once it's started there's no stopping it.'

'Oh,' I said.

She went on excitedly, 'I've been reading about the Victorians. They were mad on spiritualism! They used to have meetings where everyone would get messages from the Other Side. And their psychics used to have special little cabinets built and they'd sit in them and go into trances!'

'Oh yes?' I said doubtfully.

'And then stuff like smoke or steam would actually

come out of their mouths and form itself into the shape of the person who was being contacted – the person who was dead.'

'I've never believed that,' I said. 'I saw something about it on telly. They said it was very dark in those Victorian parlours so people couldn't see very well, and the people who were pretending to contact the dead used hidden smoke machines and bales of white floaty material. It wasn't spirit people at all! But those who came along were so anxious to trace their dead relatives that they believed everything they saw.'

Zara frowned at me.

'They found out later that the mediums had just been playing tricks. They were frauds.'

'Not all of them,' Zara said quickly. 'Some of them were really and truly psychic. And OK, some were only a bit psychic and so they got someone else – their maids – to help them along with a smoke machine or whatever they had. And if it got a bit dodgy then the psychic would go back into the cabinet and the maid would pull the curtain across and say to the audience, "Madam is sleeping now," and they'd all have to go home.'

'That would have been my job, I suppose,' I said. 'I'd have been your maid.'

Zara closed her eyes. 'I bet I could go into a trance if I tried . . .'

'Don't!' I said, alarmed. 'You might never come out of it again.'

'Or I could pretend to.' Her eyes flickered open. 'How would that look, Ella? Everyone could sit round holding hands, and I'd be sitting in the middle of the circle and I could go all woozy . . . and then I'd start talking in a strange voice. A voice from the Other Side . . .'

'I don't think you ought to,' I said, shivering. 'It wouldn't be right.'

'And then you could direct the questions and turn the lights off at the right time, and go round with the bell and everything, and say things like, "Please don't touch Zara while she's in a trance." It'd be great!'

'I'm not so sure,' I said, staring over the balcony at the bouncing ghost below us. I didn't mind ghosts like *that*: sparkly, fake ones. I didn't want any dealings with real ones, though.

'Don't be such a wimp!' she said. 'Anyway, we've got to carry on now we've started. I mean, they're all desperate for more. Everyone keeps asking me when I'm going to read the Tarot.'

'And when are you?'

'When I know a bit more about it,' she said. 'I've got a book out of the library but it's really complicated.'

I wanted to ask her – I kept wanting to ask her – more about my dad and his secret, but I thought I'd better get to the question from another angle. 'Look, I just want to get this straight,' I said. 'When you said all that about Sophie having a big secret, were you just making it up?'

She was silent for a while, then she shrugged. 'I don't really know. It's just words that come into my head. Ideas about people. I could be making them up, or they could be coming from . . . somewhere else. Who knows?'

I swallowed. 'And . . . and when you said that about my dad?'

She shrugged again.

'But how can I find out if there *is* anything?'

'Why don't you do what I do?' she said. 'Keep your eyes open and your ears flapping and perhaps you'll discover what it is before I do. Perhaps it won't be anything so bad at all.'

We'd finished our meal long ago but I pushed a remnant of chip around my plate, thinking. I didn't really *want* to find out about any secret of my dad's.

Didn't they say that ignorance was bliss? But I also knew that I wouldn't be able to help myself.

Zara wasn't thinking about my dad any more. 'Anyway, people like Sophie sometimes need something to bring them down a bit.'

I looked at her curiously.

'I mean, just look at her!' Zara suddenly spat out. 'How can anyone have that much?'

'What d'you mean?'

'Well, she's Miss Gorgeous of the Year, isn't she – she's got a perfect model figure, super-white teeth and a metre of glossy hair to flick back from her face.' Zara made an effort to flick back her own hair, but it was so matted with gel that it didn't move. I didn't know what to say. Obviously we all envied Sophie – who wouldn't want to be tall and slim and gorgeous? – but I hadn't realised that with Zara it went a bit further than this.

'She's got the perfect family, too,' she went on. 'A mum and a dad, two gorgeous little sisters – they're all straight off the front of a cornflakes packet. She's probably got a Golden Labrador puppy as well.'

I started giggling at this and after a moment Zara did too.

But in my head I felt uneasy. 'We don't have to go

on doing this stuff, do we?' I said. 'Can't we just stop?'

'You're kidding!' Zara said. 'This is our greatest hour, Ella. We're stars! We're not going to stop now.'

Chapter Six

'Do you believe in ghosts?' I asked Mum one evening the following week. Dad was out and we'd been watching a TV documentary on psychic phenomena – on ghosts, in other words – and there had been a whole bunch of people who'd claimed to have seen any amount of them. They'd seen Roman soldiers, cavaliers, monks, headless brides . . . you name it, they'd seen them.

'Of course I don't,' Mum said briskly. 'No rational person believes in ghosts.'

'But what about all those people we've just seen on the telly?'

'Some people will say anything to get themselves on TV,' she said. 'And do you notice that when people see these ghosts, they're always on their own. You never get two people together who've seen one.'

I thought about this. 'I suppose not.'

It had been an interesting programme, though – even though I'd been so spooked that I'd had to watch it mostly from behind a cushion. After they'd spoken to people in the studio, the TV company had gone to a haunted house – one of the most haunted in Britain, they said – and talked to the people who lived there, asking them about the things they saw and heard on a regular basis. These were horses' hooves on the drive outside, ghostly moaning noises, lights going on and off, things being moved from room to room and a full-blown ghost seen swooping across the landing.

The TV people had set up ghost traps inside the house with sound recorders, special meters to measure temperature drop and a camera which would go off automatically if as much as a wisp passed it by. The people who lived there had then gone away, and the machines and meters left in place for a month. When checks were made at the end of this time, though, nothing had been recorded at all. Not a whisper; not a shadow. The only noise which had been taped was found to have been caused by a mouse chewing at a sound lead.

The woman in charge of the TV show said that

this proved that really there was no such thing as ghosts or psychic phenomena. That it was just not possible to contact the spirit world. A man, though, another expert, said that the noises had resumed once the people were back in the house, and this went to show that it wasn't the house so much as the *people* who were haunted. He said it was a combination of the right people and the right house which led to psychic phenomena occurring.

'To be fair, I suppose the real answer is that no one knows whether there are any ghosts or not,' Mum said. 'But unless I actually come face to face with one, I'm not going to believe in them.'

I shivered. 'Well if you *do* see one, don't tell me about it.'

We switched over to another channel and I glanced at Mum, not knowing whether to say anything about Zara or not. It seemed an ideal opportunity, though, as Dad was out of the way.

'Zara says she's psychic,' I said. 'She saw a ghost where they used to live.'

'Oh, did she now,' Mum said, disbelief in her voice.

'No. Really. She told me ages ago about the ghost. And she keeps having feelings about things.'

Mum laughed.

'Honestly she does. I've heard her tell the girls at school stuff that no one could possibly know. They're amazed!'

Mum looked at me and shook her head. 'Ella,' she said, 'you're so gullible sometimes! Surely you can tell truth from storytelling? She's having you on!'

'Well, I thought she was at first,' I said. 'Now I'm not so sure.'

'Well, *I'm* sure!' Mum said. 'Just take my word for it. There are no such things as ghosts and people who say they've seen them are disturbed in some way.'

'Not *all* of them,' I said earnestly. 'Some people – psychics – help the police find dead bodies, don't they? At the beginning of that programme there was a woman telling the police where to find a body in the middle of the woods, and they found it just where she said.'

'Coincidence!' Mum said promptly. 'Pure luck. For every case you hear about there are probably twenty where the psychic person – the so-called psychic person – doesn't find the body they're supposed to be looking for.'

I didn't say anything else. I was confused; not sure

about anything any more. I reached into the pocket of my jeans where my tiger's eye crystal was and held on to it. It would protect me, Zara had said. From what, though, I didn't know.

We didn't go shopping on Saturday because Zara said she wanted to use that day to read up more about Tarot cards and really get into them. Apparently they were terribly complicated: so many suites, so many pictures, so many different ways of interpreting them. If you were psychic, though, Zara told me, then the correct way to read them became clear. You turned over a card with a question in your mind and then whatever was on the card would mean something to you. Like if it was a card showing a man standing with a horse, this could either mean someone was about to arrive with a message, someone was about to depart on a long journey, or someone was going to make you a gift of something valuable. It was up to you to make the right interpretation according to what was going on in your life and how you sensed things.

On Sunday Mum and Dad went out to visit one of my aunts and I was left alone in the house. I'd been making beaded wire bracelets in my room but as soon as the front door closed I put these to one side and went downstairs. I'd said to myself that I wasn't going to worry about what Zara had said, nor was I going to hunt for my dad's secret . . . but nevertheless I found myself in the sitting room making for the big wooden desk where Mum and Dad kept all their bills and papers.

I opened the drop-down flap and started rummaging through the pigeon holes, but I had no idea what I was looking for. Besides, I thought, if Dad had a secret, was it really likely that he'd keep details of it all to hand in his desk?

I looked aimlessly through gas and electricity bills, then found some receipts for meals out and looked through them, too, all the time knowing that if it was a secret that Mum didn't know about, like an affair, then there was no way he'd keep the receipts for meals where she could find them.

In the little cupboard in the footwell of the desk there was a locked door, but this had a key in so it was hardly going to contain anything top secret. I looked in, though, just in case, and found a long brown envelope with *Last Will and Testament* written on it, which scared me so utterly that I quickly shoved everything back in and locked the little door again. I was just about to investigate a wooden box containing – as far as I could remember – a lot of broken watches, when the phone rang, making me jump out of my skin as if it was a view-phone and the caller could see what I was up to.

'Ella?' said the voice when I answered. 'It's Sky here.'

I was amazed and secretly thrilled. Sky had never rung me before; I hadn't known that she had my number.

'Hi!' I said. 'What can I do for you?'

'Well, I wanted to talk to Zara, really,' she said, sounding anxious. 'But I can't get through on her number and I wondered if she was round at your house.'

'No, she's not here,' I said. So she'd only rung me because she wanted Zara. 'Is there anything in partic-ular you want her for?' I asked politely.

'Oh, I just . . .' she hesitated and it sounded as if she was putting her hand over the phone so that no one around could hear her speak, '. . . just wanted to talk to her about something. You know she's good at finding out things; doing that psychic bit. I mean, it probably sounds a bit daft, but I want to see if she knows something.'

'Oh?' I said, hoping she'd open up a bit more.

'Maybe I'll just pop round to her house. Where does she live?'

I told her.

'Where's that?'

'It's on the Crowmarsh estate. I'll take you, if you like,' I offered, and of course it wasn't that I was being especially helpful, more that I wanted to be included in whatever was going on.

'OK,' she said. 'I know where you live. I'll be round in ten minutes.'

It was more like twenty minutes, actually, which gave me time to make my hair look a bit better and try and make my room more interesting in case she came up. Looking round, I realised how extremely childish it was, how pink and flouncy, with half a dozen stuffed animals on a shelf and a toy-lion nightdress case on the bed. Zara, of course, had banished things like stuffed animals and nightdress cases from her room long ago.

I hid the toys and made a half-hearted effort to find a duvet cover that wasn't so flowery, but in the end gave up and went downstairs. I tried to ring Zara to say we were coming, but, as Sky had said, the number was unobtainable. Zara still didn't have a mobile and I thought, actually, that her mum might be in some sort of money trouble – perhaps out of work. Once, ages ago, she'd been a nurse, but then she'd got the sack and become a ward orderly and the last I'd heard she'd been a hospital cleaner. She was at home all sorts of odd hours now, though, and I hadn't liked to ask Zara if she still had a job.

When I answered the door to Sky she told me that she didn't want to come in. 'If you don't mind, can we just get round to Zara's?' she said. She seemed downcast; not her normal glowing self.

'Is it anything I can know about?' I asked as we set off walking, because I didn't want to just deposit her on Zara's doorstep and go home again.

She hesitated, then she said, 'I suppose it doesn't matter if you know or not. It's about Anton.'

'The DJ?'

She sighed. 'I really love him. I'm mad about him! He won't believe me, though. I think he's going off me.'

'Oh,' I said sympathetically. 'Why d'you think that?'

'He's gone all cold on me. Like, you know I told him I couldn't go to Paris?'

I nodded. 'I heard you weren't going.'

'Since then, everything's been a mess.' She sighed again. 'It was my own fault: first I was going, then I wasn't – I just couldn't decide and he was getting more and more annoyed about it. In the end I knew my mum and dad wouldn't let me go and I couldn't lie to them. Not about something like that.'

'So you told him you weren't going?'

'Yeah. Sophie agreed with me. She said that I'd be mad if I went; that if my mum and dad found out they'd be so angry they'd never trust me again.'

'She was probably right,' I said.

'So I told Anton that I wasn't going and he threw a huge wobbly, said I couldn't love him if I could treat him like that, and if I was such a coward all my life then I'd end up miserable and alone.'

I made consoling noises.

'And since then he's been really off me. He never rings, he turns up late – everything's changed. I do still love him, though,' she added in a small voice. 'That's why I want to talk to Zara and find out if we've got any sort of a future.'

We were at Zara's house by this time. I rang the bell and though I could hear noises inside it was ages before anyone answered. The front door, I noticed, was in a right old state and looked as if it had been kicked repeatedly by someone trying to get in.

Zara started when she saw it was us. She was wearing her usual out-of-school uniform: black T-shirt and black jeans, and she'd drawn thick black lines round her eyes. I was surprised to see that she had a brand new piercing: there was a silver stud in her eyebrow.

'You can't come in,' was the first thing she said, and she stepped outside and pulled the door behind her so that we couldn't see into the house.

I thought immediately that it must be something to do with her mum, that she was drunk. 'Sky's been trying to ring you,' I said. 'And I tried as well.'

'The phone's out of order,' Zara said.

'Have you reported it?' Sky asked. 'D'you want me to do it for you when I get home?'

An odd look crossed Zara's face. 'No, don't bother,' she said after a moment. 'It's not working because the bill hasn't been paid. Mum . . . Mum forgot to do it yesterday.'

No one knew what to say to this because it so obviously wasn't true. From inside the house came a noise: laughter – a drunken sort of laughter – but we pretended not to hear it.

'Sky just wanted to ask you something,' I said.

Zara tried to look interested; her face did brighten a little.

'It's about Anton,' Sky said, looking embarrassed at the situation. 'I've been worrying and worrying and I thought of you and knew you'd be able to tell me the truth.'

The laughter from the house was getting more and more hysterical and now it seemed to be turning to crying. I felt sorry for Zara, actually. Here was Sky on her doorstep wanting to know something, asking for help, and she couldn't let her in.

'If it's difficult with your mum . . .' I lowered my voice, '. . . being drunk and everything, you can come back to my house if you like. My mum and dad are out.'

Zara nodded. It was cold out but she didn't bother to get a jacket or even shout goodbye; just pulled the door shut behind her and pushed past us down the path.

'Zara!' we heard faintly from behind us. 'Zara! Come back!'

But she didn't. She just walked on in front of us, very quickly.

We talked about all sorts of rubbish on the way

back to mine – anything to keep the conversation going, because I think we were all embarrassed. Zara told us about the piercing which she'd had done at some funny old tattoo place in town and I wondered how she'd got the money for it. Her dad sent her pocket money occasionally, though, so I suppose she might have used that.

I listened to the way she directed the chat, steering the topic around to whatever she wanted to know and hardly ever giving anything of herself away. She asked about Sophie a couple of times. First she wanted to know where Sophie was, and Sky said she wasn't sure; that they didn't usually see each other on Sundays, then she wanted to know what Sophie thought about Anton.

'Well, she's not that keen on him, actually,' Sky said. 'It's funny, really. Usually we fancy the same type of guy, but she's never got on that well with Anton. They're always having digs at each other.'

'Oh, really,' Zara said. 'And is Sophie seeing any-one at the moment?'

'She's always seeing someone!' Sky said. 'I can't keep up with her.'

We were in my bedroom by then: Sky was sitting on my one chair and Zara and I were sprawled on the flowery duvet cover. I was glad that I'd stuffed all the toys down the side of the bed before I'd gone out.

Zara looked round my room. 'I didn't think to bring anything with me to address the spirits with,' she said. 'Not my Tarot cards or my dowsing pendulum or anything.' She stood up and started looking along my bookshelves. 'Have you got anything I can use to dowse with?'

Sky looked at me curiously.

'To dowse you need something hanging on a string or a line,' I explained. 'A crystal bead or a ring or something. You ask a question and it goes one way for yes and the other way for no.' I pulled my tiger's eye out of my pocket. 'Can you use this?' I asked Zara, though I knew she couldn't really, because it didn't have a hole in it.

She didn't bother to answer me, just clasped her hands together and looked at Sky really seriously. 'What is it that you want to ask?'

Sky took a breath. Her blue eyes looked shiny, as if they were full of tears. 'I want to ask if Anton really loves me. I mean, I know it sounds ditsy but I'm so mad on him that I can't think straight. If he's gone off me I don't know what I'll do.'

Zara looked at her for a moment. 'I think I'll go into a trance,' she said. 'See what comes through.'

I sat up, startled. She hadn't tried anything like this before. In fact, we'd only talked about it once, and that had been when she'd told me about the Victorian spiritualists.

'Wow,' Sky said. 'Can you really do that?'

'Sure,' Zara said.

We didn't have a bell or anything to cleanse the room, so Zara opened the window wide and said some sort of mumbo-jumbo in front of it – something about cleansing winds and free spirits which I thought she was just making up as she went along. I had two white candles and we lit these, then Zara took over the straight chair and sat in it, perfectly still, her head fallen forward and her eyes closed.

Sky and I sat on the bed and looked at each other. I really had no idea what was going to happen. Nothing *did* happen for ages, then Zara kind of shivered all over and said in a high, faraway voice, 'Spirits of the upper air! We come in peace and seek your guidance. Please give us the answer to a question.'

Sky clutched my hand, looking utterly amazed, seeming to be taken in by everything, and I . . . well, I thought Zara was probably just mucking around but it all sounded so eerie and weird that I couldn't help feeling scared.

'Ask the question,' Zara intoned.

'Does Anton love me?' Sky said.

Zara shook a little, as if she was freezing cold, and then lifted her head. Still with her eyes closed she said in the same faraway voice, 'No. He loves another.'

'Oh!' Sky clasped her hand to her mouth. 'Oh, no!'

I wanted to say to her that it might not be true, that Zara was probably only having a bit of a joke, but I didn't dare say anything at all because it so clearly wasn't a joke to Sky.

Zara gave a small gasp and seemed about to say more, but then her eyes suddenly shot open and she stared ahead of her. 'No!' she cried.

'What's the matter?' I asked, because she sounded completely terrified.

'There's something evil around this house!' She stood up, rushed to the window and started taking in big gulps of air. 'Some bad spirit!'

'*What?*' I cried.

'Some awful thing . . . This house is in the grip of a dark secret!'

And, leaving me and Sky just sitting there, horrified, Zara ran down the stairs and out of the door.

Chapter Seven

'I tell you, I can't remember,' Zara said as we walked into school together. 'Yesterday afternoon is all kind of hazy. I can't remember *what* I said when I was at your house. I was in a trance.'

I glared at her. I felt like having a real go at her, actually, for what she was putting me through; for the sleepless night I'd had and for the horrible kicked feeling in my stomach. 'You can't just go round saying things like that, saying things about people's houses being evil . . .'

'Did I actually say *that*?' she asked incredulously.

'Something like it. Something about my house being in the grip of a terrible secret.'

'I can't remember. Honestly,' she looked at me wide-eyed. 'I was kind of semi-conscious. That's what happens when you go into a trance.'

'Oh really?'

'Someone – something – took me over. I can't remember anything about it, what I said or who I spoke about.' She looked at me intently. 'What did I actually say to Sky?'

'You told her that her boyfriend doesn't love her. That he loves someone else.'

'Did I say who that someone was?'

I shook my head. We were getting off the subject. Sure, I was interested in Sky and her romance, but I was more interested in my house and my family. *Some awful thing*, Zara had said. *A dark secret . . .*

'How long was I in a trance?'

I sighed heavily. 'You must know. You *do* know! You're just saying all this, aren't you? Just pretending you were in a trance to try and impress everyone.'

'I'm not!'

I'd started walking again by this time and she caught me up and put her arm through mine. 'Honestly, Ella. I wouldn't deliberately say something like that to upset you. You know I wouldn't!'

'Do I?'

'You're my best mate. We're a team!' I didn't reply and she squeezed my arm. 'Of course we are. We'd be nothing without each other, would we?'

I still didn't say anything.

'You're the best friend I ever had. My mate! We don't need any of those others, do we?'

I thought I could just about see where she was coming from here. Did she think that I was going to go off with someone else? With The Four? Well, as if *that* was going to happen . . .

'You really can't remember anything, then?' I asked, beginning to unbend a little. 'Anything else about what happened and what you said about my house?'

'I can't! But honestly, even if I said something about bad spirits, it's probably nothing at all. Mischievous little spirits can mess up all sorts of things, and if the room isn't cleansed properly and the vibes are wrong they can turn everything haywire. I'm sure there's nothing wrong really in your house.'

'But you said something before about my dad.'

She spread her hands. 'It's probably nothing. It was just a *feeling*. I can't help my feelings, can I?'

We didn't speak for a while and then I glanced at her eyebrow, which looked red and swollen. There was no stud or ring in it because we weren't allowed to have them at school. 'Is that all right?' I asked, pointing to it. 'It looks a bit raw.'

'It'll be OK,' she said dismissively, feeling with her fingers along the raised flesh.

'What made you have another one? What did your mum say?'

She shrugged; looked away from me. 'She didn't notice.'

Too drunk, I thought. Or too something. Disinterested, maybe.

'Is your mum OK?' I asked suddenly.

'Yeah,' she replied sharply. 'Why shouldn't she be?'

'Well, I wondered why you . . . you know, wouldn't let us in.' I wasn't probing, really. Well, maybe I was, but I wasn't doing it to be nasty. I was doing it in case Zara wanted to talk to me about her mum and her problems.

'We'd just had a bit of a row, that was all,' she said in a niggly voice. 'It was nothing. She wasn't drunk! I wish you hadn't said that in front of Sky.'

'Oh, well, sorry,' I said, shrugging. 'I didn't think.' So if her mum hadn't been drunk, then what had all that laughing and crying been about?

'What did you and Sky do after I left?' Zara asked as we went into our tutor room. 'Did she stay round at yours chatting for ages and ages?'

'Not really,' I said.

'I bet your dad likes *her*, doesn't he?'

I shot her a glance. 'He didn't see her. She was gone by the time they got back.'

'Oh. Did she talk about Anton and what I'd said?'

'Of course she did. She didn't talk about anything else.'

And that was lucky for me, really, because she'd been so devastated about the Anton business that she'd hardly registered what Zara had said about my house having a dark secret. Maybe she'd just thought that was an elaborate bit of staging. All she'd wanted to talk about was Anton; had he ever loved her? Did he really have someone else? Would she get him back? She'd asked me not to say anything to any of the others, and I'd promised I wouldn't.

At break that morning, though, it was obvious that her own little crowd knew, because they were fluttering about and making a big fuss of her, saying that he must be mad not to want to go out with her, and it was his loss, and all those other things you say to your friend when she's been given the elbow. I thought it was odd that she hadn't actually spoken to Anton yet and asked him what was going on, though. I wanted to tell her not to jump the gun; to say that we didn't know that Zara was right, didn't know for *sure* that she was psychic, but I could hardly barge through everyone and bleat it out. Besides, it would have sounded so disloyal to Zara, seeing as I was her so-called psychic assistant.

Anyway, in some odd way, Sky seemed to be enjoying the drama of it all. She had Sophie, Poppy and Lois beside her, cooing and sympathising, telling her that blokes were all the same and that they'd thought all along that he was too good to be true.

'You and he weren't really suited anyway,' Sophie said.

When we went over to them, Sky gave Poppy a little push to one side to allow Zara through to the inner circle. 'Here's my guru!' she said. She looked round at everyone. 'Really, Zara was just so *amazing*. I asked her the question about Anton and she just went all weird and . . .' she pulled a zombie-like attitude, '. . . came out with the answer!'

Everyone exclaimed and marvelled a bit, and Zara shrugged and said it was nothing and anyway, she'd been in a trance and couldn't remember what had happened. Then Sky said, 'What d'you think I ought to do now?'

'About what?' Zara asked.

'Well, should I finish with him properly, seeing as I know he's going to finish with me?' She looked down and sighed. 'I know I sound strong now but honestly I'm *heartbroken*.'

'I don't really want to suggest what you should do next,' Zara said, 'but I brought my Tarot cards in. We could see what they say if you like.'

I looked at her in surprise because she hadn't told me she was bringing the cards in and we hadn't arranged any sort of scam with them, but in some ways I was relieved not to be involved in it. It wasn't just Sky who wanted to have her Tarot cards read – a load of others did, too – so Zara said that after lunch she'd just let everyone cut the pack once, see what card they got and then give her interpretation of it.

'I'm not saying it'll be a hundred per cent accurate or that I'm always right or anything,' she said. 'I don't want to get the blame if you act on what you find out and then it all goes wrong.' And then everyone said they didn't mind that and that they just wanted to have their fortunes told.

At lunchtime that day there was a music group practising in our tutor room, so we went outside to one of the wooden benches that stood in front of the school's reception area. There were nine of us altogether: the same little crowd that had come along to the psychometric thing, plus a girl called Jenna. Sophie was there, of course, making a great fuss about not wanting to go and having to be literally dragged there by Sky and Poppy.

I think some other girls really wanted to be included, but because it was The Four most of them kept a respectful distance, hoping (as I'd often done) that someone might invite them along. As before, everyone was quite excited, partly because it was just something different and partly because we were all wondering what Zara was going to come up with next.

I couldn't go round with the bell in four corners seeing as we were outside, but Zara said it would be enough to shake the bell in the air a few times, so I did this. Then she carefully took out the pack of Tarot cards, which had been wrapped up in a square of purple velvet. She said that you had to be careful how you put them away because it could be bad for one card to lie next to one that opposed it.

She shuffled the cards carefully. 'Look, I've hardly done this before,' she said as we all gathered around her, 'and I'm not even sure of all the meanings, so if it's just a meaningless load of rubbish . . .'

'It won't be!' Sky said. 'She's fantastic,' she assured the others, then added sadly, 'I only wish she wasn't.'

One by one we took it in turns to sit next to Zara and cut the cards.

I went first. She put the pack down on the bench between us and I picked up a wedge of cards and showed her the one underneath. On it was a woman standing under a tree, with a stream running by. I was a bit apprehensive, scared that she was going to say something scary again, but she said it was a lovely card to have, one of the nicest, and the stream meant that any worries that I might have would flow away and the tree meant I would be sheltered from anything bad happening.

Poppy went next – something about a meeting with a stranger; then Lois, who was told she would receive something about her future through the post. Sky, still looking forlorn, sat down next and Zara frowned at the card she'd chosen.

Sky gave an agonised sigh. 'Not more bad news!'

'No,' Zara said. 'It just confirms things. Look.' She held up the card, which showed three people in a dark, tangled wood. One figure was in the foreground, the other two stood behind him with masks over their faces.

'Three people in a wood,' Sky said.

Zara nodded. 'Exactly. The eternal triangle. This figure, in front, stands for Anton.' She pointed first to one figure, then the next. 'And this one here is you . . . and this is your rival in love.'

Sky gasped, so did some of the others. 'It's so spooky that you should get that exact card!' India said.

'Does it say . . . I mean, do I get any guidance about what I should do?' Sky asked breathlessly.

Zara shook her head. 'This is just the situation as it stands. It's up to you to make use of it as you will. I mean . . .' Her eyes flickered over the rest of the girls. 'It all depends on your rival, really; who she is, how clever she is, how determined she is to hold on to Anton. Do you want to put up a fight for him, or do you want to just let him go?'

'Hang on,' Sophie said. 'Aren't you jumping the gun a bit? I mean, Sky hasn't even spoken to Anton about all this yet. Suppose you've got it all wrong.'

Zara looked at her steadily. 'I haven't.'

There was a pause, a very loaded, silent pause. I was thinking about my card and wondering if Zara had made all that stuff up, then became aware that she and Sophie were staring each other out.

'Oh, come on!' India said suddenly, looking at her watch. 'The rest of us are waiting to have our go and we've only got ten minutes!' Laughing, she pulled Sky out of the seat next to Zara and sat herself down instead.

Zara shuffled and India cut the cards. She'd chosen a woman sitting on a chair, which could have been a throne, with several people surrounding her.

'This is something to do with your domestic life,' Zara said. 'It could be a holiday together or a celebration coming up.'

India beamed. 'Spot on!' she said. 'It's my gran's birthday and we're giving her a big party.'

Everyone clapped, then Sophie muttered something about it all being stupid and having something better to do with her time. She said she wasn't going to hang about any longer.

Sky grabbed hold of her, holding her back. 'No, come on, don't be a spoilsport!' she said. 'You can go next.' And Sophie was pushed into the hot seat.

She sat there sulkily, shaking her head so that her hair flicked backwards and forwards across her face. 'This is crazy,' she said. 'I don't know what I'm *doing* here. I don't believe a word of it.'

'Sophie!' Sky said. 'Lighten up. It's just a bit of

fun. And who knows what you'll find out.'

Sophie stuck her lip out moodily, but cut the deck and showed the card to Zara without looking to see what it was herself.

Zara stared at it and a funny expression came over her face: triumph, cunning . . . I wasn't quite sure what it was. She then held it out to the rest of us and we all saw that it was exactly the same card that Sky had chosen.

There was a moment's silence.

'What does *that* mean?' Sky said then, clearly startled. 'Have we chosen the same card because we're best friends or something?'

Sophie looked at the card for the first time, shrugged, went to say something and thought better of it.

'Wow!' someone else said.

'Would you like to say what it means, Sophie?' Zara asked quietly.

Sophie looked contemptuous. 'How the hell should I know?' she said rudely. 'It's just some card with three people on it. Three people in a wood. What am I supposed to say about that?'

Zara had a small, tight smile on her face. 'These situations are difficult, I know,' she said. 'Especially when it's your best friend.'

I was puzzled, looking at the small twitch which had started up at the side of Sophie's mouth, but didn't read any more into it. I obviously couldn't be at all psychic or I would have realised what Zara was getting at; *had* been getting at for some days now.

'This is you, isn't it?' Zara said to Sophie suddenly. 'You're the other figure in the triangle.'

Sophie flung back the hair from her face in a dramatic gesture. 'Whoa! What is this? You're crazy.'

'I'm not at all,' Zara said. 'I'm just speaking the truth. You and Anton . . . are an item.' There was a little scream from Sky and a collective intake of breath from everyone else.

'You might just as well admit it,' Zara went on. 'I knew you had a secret, but I wasn't sure what it was. Now I know. We all know.'

'It's not true!' Sophie said. 'It's utter rubbish!'

Sky's eyes filled with tears. 'Oh, Sophie! That's why you kept telling me not to go to Paris! And where you've been going those evenings we haven't seen each other . . . and why you tried to put me off him!'

'No, no, no!' Sophie interrupted. 'It's not true, I tell you!'

'It is! It all falls into place now!' Sky cried. 'You're just a wicked, two-faced cow! How could you do that to me, Sophie! You're supposed to be my friend!'

'Oh, you believe her, do you?' Sophie said. 'Believe that trouble-making bitch over me!'

And so it went on: first one, then the other, while we just stood there staring at each of them in turn, at the two girls who'd been best friends in all the world suddenly reduced to slagging each other off.

None of us knew what to say or do for the best. Should we comfort Sky? Back up Sophie? Pretend it wasn't our business and just drift away?

The bell went and we still stood there making raised-eyebrow faces at each other. Only Zara seemed in control of the situation; calm, all-seeing and all-knowing. She finished folding the cards into the purple velvet and then gave me a meaningful look, nodding towards the school for us to go indoors.

'*Now* let's see what happens,' she whispered in my ear as we walked away.

Chapter Eight

'Is it true?' I said to Zara as we went into school. 'Is it really true about Sophie and Anton?'

'Probably,' she said, shrugging carelessly. 'That's what came through.'

'But –'

'I'm the messenger and that's the message I got. I just passed it on.' She ran her finger along her eyebrow, touching the swelling around the new piercing, which looked now as if it might have gone a bit poisonous.

'But should you have *told*? I mean, it's all a bit drastic, isn't it?'

'Everyone wants to know things about their life,' she said.

'Yes, but –'

'All I do is tell them. They pick the cards; I just interpret them. If they're not prepared to find out stuff, they shouldn't ask me in the first place.'

'Oh.' It was pitifully inadequate, but I didn't know what else to say. It just hadn't seemed right, somehow, to just come out with such a devastating thing as Zara had done. It felt to me as if it was upsetting the order of things; interfering too much with people's lives.

Word of what had happened to Sky and Sophie spread through the rest of the class. We had Games next and in the changing rooms everyone gathered in little groups discussing it, putting their opinions forward, saying it was disgusting, marvelling how Sophie could do that to Sky, saying how Sky would be beside herself . . .

What no one did was question what Zara had said. That was just taken as the perfect truth.

Sky wasn't in the changing rooms and word came back that someone had seen her walking across the playground towards the school gates. Sophie didn't turn up until we were in our sports kit and just about to go outside for a jog, and when she did everyone just kind of froze, waiting to see how she'd act and if she'd say anything.

She didn't say a word, though. She just came up to Zara and, with all the rest of us still goggling, *slapped her round the face*!

There were a couple of gasps and cries from everyone. Imagine being slapped round the face by the most popular girl in the class! I knew Zara had a temper so I waited, breath held, to see what she'd do next, to see if this was going to be the first blow struck in a big brawl. Zara hardly reacted to the slap at all, though. She just stood there with a funny half-smile on her face and said, 'You'll pay for that.'

That was all. I got the feeling that she'd somehow won the round, though.

We all went off on a run – apart from Sophie, I think she stayed inside – but as soon as we got out of sight of our games teacher we gathered in little gossiping groups to talk about what had happened and what might be going to happen. We talked of nothing else for the rest of that afternoon, and Zara and I became the most sought-after girls in the class. They bombarded us – well, Zara mostly – with questions. *How long did she think it had been going on? Did she think Sophie would go to Paris with him now? She'd said ages ago that Sophie had a secret; had she known what it was? Did she think they'd ever be friends again?*

No one was quite sure what to do about Sophie, whether to snub her or what. I think that anyone else who'd done what she'd done – what we *thought* she'd done – would have been snubbed, but she and Sky had been Most Popular for so long that it was impossible for Sophie to lose her status just like that. When all was said and done she was still extremely pretty, still had the longest, blondest hair and was still clever and sophisticated.

Four o'clock came, everyone gathered on the gravel for the bus and there was still no sign of Sky, so everyone decided that she *must* have gone home. The bus came and we all got on, but no one sat in the back seat, not even Sophie. She sat with India in the middle of the bus and – so those around her reported – never said a word.

Jenna and Chloe, who hadn't managed to cut the Tarot cards in all the Sophie/Sky excitement, came up to Zara and asked if she could do a reading for them the next day.

'Maybe not tomorrow,' Zara said, pretending to fan herself. 'I've got psychic overload. I don't want to overdo it.'

'Well, whenever you can,' Chloe said, sounding respectful. 'When you feel like it.'

'She's going to try and contact my mum for me soon,' I heard Lois telling Chloe as she moved further down the bus. 'I might even be able to speak to her.'

'So what's psychic overload?' I asked Zara.

'It just means that I'd like to get the Sophie and Sky business over with before I drop any more bombshells.'

'*Are* there any more bombshells?'

She grinned at me and raised her eyebrows.

I bit my lip. 'Don't you think . . . aren't you concerned about what's happened?' I asked. 'Aren't you worried about how you've split them up?'

'Why should I be?' she asked, sounding surprised. 'I haven't done anything wrong.'

'But if you hadn't told in the first place . . .'

'If I hadn't said anything then Sky would have carried on not knowing.'

'Maybe that would have been best,' I said, half to myself.

'Anyway,' she went on. 'There's Chloe. That'll be more trouble.'

'What d'you mean? How d'you know that?' I asked, startled.

'There's something about her aura which isn't quite right.'

This didn't mean a thing to me and I frowned, trying to remember what had happened when we'd been doing the psychometry thing and Zara had held

Chloe's silver ring. As far as I could remember, Zara had just said something about the person who'd given her the ring not being around any more, and I'd forgotten about it afterwards because of the more dramatic happening with Lois.

'Is there something awful going on with Chloe, then?' I asked.

'You'll see,' she said, and there was a sly note in her voice which I hadn't heard before. 'You'll all just have to wait and see.'

It was different now, on the bus. Quiet. Fragile. Everyone was looking at Sophie and whispering behind their hands. There was no giggling – and certainly no singing. I stared down at my hands and said, 'Do you sometimes wish you hadn't started it all?'

Zara looked at me as if I was half-cooked. 'Are you crazy?' she said. 'These last weeks have been the best ever. I'm positively famous across school. We're somebodies, Ella! Everyone wants to know us.'

'But all this – all the psychic bit. I didn't think it was going to be like this,' I said, for it seemed to me that somehow we'd moved from just playing a game to being in deadly earnest. 'I thought you were just going to tell people what their favourite colours were and whether their boyfriends' star signs were the right match for theirs. That sort of messing-about stuff.'

'Per-lease,' Zara said, rolling her eyes. 'I consider myself a bit more talented than that.'

The bus pulled up at my stop. When I got off and called goodbye, it sounded to me as if nearly everyone on the bus answered.

I walked the short distance home trying to smooth down my hair a little. It had been raining, though, which had turned it into a mess of fluffiness. I was smoothing it down because I'd seen a nice-looking guy around and was really hoping to see him again. He was quite tall – I referred to him as 'Lofty' in my head – and had very fair, almost blond hair. I thought he might have moved into the block of flats at the end of our road.

Despite walking as slowly as I could I didn't see him around that day, though, so had to be content with just daydreaming about him. At least, I thought, I knew for a fact that no one in our class lived in those flats, so I had a good chance of getting to him before anyone else did. Maybe, maybe, it would develop into something . . .

* * *

'I saw Zara's mum in town today,' Mum said that evening. We were in the sitting room; she and Dad were watching some boring old news programme and, through sheer laziness, I hadn't managed to get myself off the sofa and upstairs to my room.

I shot a look at Dad, wishing that Mum wouldn't start talking about Zara or her mum when Dad was around, because it was bound to lead to aggro.

'Oh yes?' I said.

'In a bit of a state, she was.'

I didn't say anything.

'Sitting on the wall outside the pub.'

'No harm in that,' I said.

'And singing!' Mum added.

Dad gave an ohdearwhatevernext kind of heavy sigh.

'I've seen *you* drunk before now!' I said to him, wondering if that was the sort of secret Zara had hinted at. Something like him being drunk? But she'd talked about *evil*. Something evil in the house, she'd said . . .

'You haven't seen me drunk in public,' Dad retorted. 'I've not been drunk in the road. And you certainly haven't seen your mother drunk. Disgusting, that is.'

'Why's that worse than a man being drunk, then?' I asked.

He didn't reply.

'Well, anyway –' I began.

'*Well!*' Dad corrected me. 'Speak properly, please.'

I groaned. 'Well,' I said, accentuating the 'l's to the point of absurdity, 'if her mum's a lush it's hardly Zara's fault.'

'No, it's not her fault,' Dad said, 'but you can see why I don't like you associating with her, can't you?'

'But that's not fair,' I said, and I should have got up and flounced to my room then, but I guess I was feeling too lazy. Either that or I didn't feel like defending Zara just at that moment.

Later, up in my room, I started to think about secrets and remembered how I'd once ruined Christmas for myself. I'd been about eight and had stopped believing in Father Christmas. I knew Mum had various secrets and that they were mostly to do with me: I'd been out shopping with her and seen things hurriedly wrapped and shoved to the bottom of her bag, I'd heard her on the phone ordering stuff and had seen parcels being pushed into temporary hiding places. I *knew* there were presents around and was desperate to know what they were.

I was hardly ever alone in the house, though. Mum told me once that, having waited so long for a second child, they'd rather wrapped me up in cotton wool. But I waited and waited and, when my brother was out with his mates and Mum was busy downstairs, I crept upstairs and looked for likely places to do a more thorough search when I had the opportunity.

One day I got my chance. It was pouring with rain, Dad phoned from somewhere for a lift home and, as I was deep in a TV programme and had a bad cold, Mum didn't want to take me out with her. Toby wasn't around, so I promised Mum that I wouldn't budge from the TV or answer the door for the half hour she would be gone.

It was just what I'd been waiting for. The moment her car drove off down the road I set my watch alarm for twenty-five minutes like I was on *Mission Impossible* or something, and started trawling through all the hiding places I'd previously thought of: at the back of the sideboard, in the bottom drawer of the desk, in a dusty old crate in the broom cupboard, behind all the clothes in the wardrobes and in the suitcases under the bed. Under the stairs I found a box containing presents that were obviously meant for Toby – boys' things – but I couldn't find mine.

With four minutes to go I was getting desperate, and then I thought of the top shelf of the airing cupboard. I got a chair from my bedroom, pulled it into the hall and, stretching right up, just managed to reach the edge of an old duvet cover.

They were there! I can still remember the thrill of feeling that cover full of lumpy, bumpy objects, *loads* of them. Dragging it off its shelf and on to the floor I hurriedly opened it and found a Barbie, two books, an expensive game I'd asked for, a new watch, some videos, a soft toy that spoke, a flower-pressing set and a whole load of other little stocking presents. I trawled through the lot and then I stuffed everything back into the duvet cover and shoved it back on the shelf. All in all, it had taken about a minute to look at everything.

No one ever found out. I never told. But on Christmas morning when I reached for the pillowcase on the end of my bed there was no thrill or excitement. In fact, I burst into tears when I realised there were no surprises, that my Christmas was stale and spoilt and that it was all my fault.

So – what was I thinking? That it was better not to know things? That Sky, if she hadn't found out about Sophie, might have gone on seeing Anton until they'd broken up naturally when he'd gone back to France? That at least would have preserved the best-friendship between her and Sophie.

And what about my dad's secret? Suppose I found it out and it ruined our lives? What about Chloe? What of the seance where Lois was going to contact her mum? Would knowing any of that stuff make us happier?

Maybe it was better if secrets stayed just that.

Chapter Nine

I didn't go out with Zara that Saturday because my brother came home from uni for the weekend and – big surprise – asked me if I wanted to go with him to Sweet Sounds, this really cool second-hand CD shop in town.

This was fine by me – *great*, in fact, because I hardly ever got to spend time with him – but I'd already arranged to meet Zara. I told Toby this, thinking that maybe she could come with us.

He groaned. 'Not her,' he said. 'Anyone but her.'

'She's my best friend!' I protested.

'I'm amazed you're still going round with her.'

'God, you're such a snob!' I said, giving him a shove. 'You're just like Dad.'

'It's not being a snob, Ella. Or maybe it is,' he grinned, 'but she does look a bit pikey, you must admit.'

'Don't be so horrible!' I protested, but of course I did know what he meant. I quite fancied going out with him on my own, anyway, so on the Friday I told Zara that my brother was around and we were going out as a family, so I wouldn't be able to meet her. She was OK about it; she didn't sound as if she minded.

I did see her in town that morning, actually, but she didn't see me. Toby and I had spent a couple of hours in Sweet Sounds and had been walking back home when I'd spotted her on the other side of the road in a crowd of shoppers.

'Oh look, there's Zara,' I said to Toby, nodding towards her.

Toby looked and made a barking noise. 'What a state!' he said, and he dragged me into a shop doorway to hide until she'd gone by.

I felt a bit bad to be hiding from her, but I had to say she *did* look grim. She was wearing possibly the shortest skirt ever, plus huge army boots with great thick woolly socks. She had black lipstick and her hair was hanging all over the place.

'She's gone Goth,' I said as we watched her going up the road.

'Half-Goth, half-dog,' Toby said, which made me laugh, though it shouldn't have really.

*　　*　　*

'When you do the seance, will I actually be able to speak to my mum?' Lois asked one day the following week. 'Will she have messages for me?'

'I don't know,' Zara said. 'I can't choose who comes through. It all depends whether your mum wants to contact you or not on that particular day. If she does, she'll make her presence felt.'

Funny, I thought. She was speaking about it so easily, making it sound as if contacting the dead was something she could do as easily as getting someone on the phone. She must have been reading up on how to do it.

I looked at Lois. Her expression was really wistful, almost sad, and I wondered again if what Zara was doing was right. Or even if it was genuine.

It was the Monday following the Sky and Sophie disclosure and half the class were sitting around waiting for the other half to come in and talking about what had happened. Had Sky and Sophie seen each other over the weekend and had a full-scale row? we wondered. Had Sky been to see Anton? Had Anton been to see Sophie?

Various rumours spread about the place: someone swore they'd seen Sophie at the mainline station catching a train to London, someone else said they'd seen Sky out with Anton, shopping and looking in a jeweller's window. This was *so* not true that we started laughing, and then the stories got more and more wild: Sophie had been seen snogging Anton, Sophie and Sky had been seen rolling round the floor fighting in the hairdresser's, Sky had been seen buying a wedding dress . . .

It was the number one topic of conversation. And when that flagged then the number two topic was Zara and her skills.

'Don't forget you're going to do the Tarot cards for me,' Chloe said, draping her arm around Zara's shoulders. 'Can't we do it now – before class?'

Zara shook her head. 'It can't all be done in a rush,' she said, and I knew what she really meant. She couldn't do it there and then because she liked to build things up and set the scene. She was now a *psychic*, a person of great importance. And besides, since she'd hinted that Chloe had something interesting going on in her life, she obviously wanted an audience around to marvel at her pronouncements.

Sky eventually came in, looking a bit subdued, and everyone made a great fuss about saying hello to her and asking what sort of a weekend she'd had. Poppy went to sit next to her, they had a hurried, whispered talk and then both went outside. We all looked at each other – where had they gone? – and then someone peered around the door and saw that they were moving all Sky's things to a spare locker further along the row, away from Sophie's locker.

This was all amazing and startling. I mean, Sky and Sophie had been best, closest, most intimate friends for *years*. And now that friendship was all over.

Sophie came in while they were outside, so she must have had to walk right past them. She looked really good, actually. Her hair was straighter and glossier than ever and she'd had her school skirt shortened drastically so that her legs looked amazingly long underneath it. They looked browner, too – I knew she and her family belonged to a health club so she'd obviously been on a tanning bed at the weekend. Lois went over to Sophie and they went into a little huddle.

After a moment Sky came back in with Poppy and everyone in the class simply *stared* at them, wondering what was going to happen. All that did, though, was that Poppy and Sky stayed sitting together and so did Lois and Sophie.

*   *   *

A couple of days went by and it was really odd to see how everything had changed. From being the absolute centre of everything, the source of most of the laughs we had in class and all the gossip and giggles, Sky and Sophie had become outsiders. Everything had depended on The Two; we all took our lead from them. If we had a supply teacher and they liked her, then everyone liked her. If they were keen on the particular book we were doing in English Lit, then everyone was keen on it. I'm not saying that some of us didn't have opinions of our own or that we trailed around after them like puppies, but it was just that we trusted their judgement. They were so attractive, confident and all the rest that if *they* thought a particular way, then everyone knew it was OK – even preferable – to think that way too.

Now it was all different. Sophie and Sky were subdued, so the rest of the class was subdued as well. The Two were no more, and The Four were no more either. Poppy and Lois hadn't fallen out, but they might just as well have done, because Sophie refused to acknowledge Poppy when she was with Sky, and Sky did the same with Lois when she was with Sophie.

Occasionally, little bits of news drifted back to the

rest of us: Sky had texted Anton, told him she never wanted to see him again and was now refusing to answer her phone when she saw it was from him; Sky had said she hated Sophie and would never be friends with her again *ever*; Sophie hated Sky and had said it was no wonder that Anton had gone off her.

I didn't know what to believe. But what I did know was that it was all horrible.

And the strange thing was that now that Zara and I were in the middle of everything, it wasn't so important to be there. The whole dynamics of the class had changed. The Two weren't The Two any longer.

Zara read the Tarot cards for Jenna and Chloe a few days later in our tutor room at lunchtime. She'd already added an enhancement to her routine before she started a reading: apart from having me sound the bell to cleanse the room, she now said she had to *centre* herself. This meant, apparently, that she had to have a moment's silence from everyone to enable her to 'draw light and energy down and get in touch with her psychic side'.

Hearing she was doing this centring, everyone went as quiet as mice, taking it very seriously indeed. And of course Sophie wasn't around now to throw the occasional spanner in the works by saying she didn't believe in it. She, someone told us, now went into the library at lunchtimes and had also joined the drama club.

Zara started off by reading Jenna's cards, but didn't come out with anything really interesting, just said things like she loved surprises, had a touch of the wild child about her but kept it well hidden, and would like to live somewhere more exciting. She could have said the same thing, I realised, to more or less anyone in class.

She made much more of Chloe's reading, saying that she would do her something called a 'cosmic triple'. Chloe had to fan all the cards face down and mix them around on the desk top, then gather them together into a pack again and turn over the first three cards. Zara said that these, in order, represented Chloe's past, present and future.

She studied these three for some time without saying anything, then asked Chloe if she had any particular question to ask.

'Yes – when am I going to meet a really fit guy?' said Chloe.

'I don't think that sort of relationship is showing up here,' Zara said, still looking at the cards. 'So you're probably not about to meet anyone important – at least not in the next year.'

Chloe stuck out her bottom lip, pretending to look peeved.

'But there are some interesting things going on in your life,' Zara continued.

'Tell me!' Chloe said.

Zara gave a slight smile. 'Well, take this one . . . your past.' She pointed to Chloe's first card, which was of a group of people standing beside a lake. 'This looks like you and your family embarking on a holiday. Or a big move, perhaps?'

Chloe nodded slowly. 'Yeah. I know what that was.' We all knew, actually, that Chloe and her family had been set to go to Canada to live, and had then changed their minds. Or that's what she'd told us.

'And this second card shows the reason you didn't go . . .'

There was a picture showing someone isolated, on the top of a hill.

Chloe shrugged. 'Does it?'

Zara nodded and closed her eyes, as if thinking deeply. 'You didn't go to Canada because of your brother.'

Chloe didn't say anything. We all looked at each

other and made raised-eyebrow faces. What was she on about?

'Your brother was convicted of something and he's in prison, isn't he?' Zara went on bluntly, and we all gasped in surprise.

Chloe flushed a deep pink. 'No!' she said indignantly. 'No, he isn't in prison.'

'I think he is.'

'He's not!'

'The plans to live abroad got cancelled because of him going inside. And of course they won't ever let you in now because he's got a criminal record.'

For a moment Chloe looked as if she was about to burst into tears, but then she composed herself, stood up and glared at Zara. 'Well, thanks very much for letting everyone know that, Zara,' she said. 'But actually, he's not in prison, he's in a Young Offenders' Institution.'

'Same thing,' Zara said, shrugging slightly. She looked down at the third card. 'You don't want to know about your future, then?' she said, but Chloe had gone out, slamming the door behind her.

Zara bent over and rested her palms gently on the floor – to *earth* herself, she explained; to bring herself back to earth after being in touch with her higher self. And then the bell went and everyone disappeared pretty quickly. Another scandal to talk about.

I asked Zara on the way home how she'd known. I mean, to me those cards wouldn't have meant anything – a group of people beside water, someone up a mountain. How could they have added up to the things she'd said?

'That's just the difference between being normal and being psychic,' Zara said. 'I told you way back there was something funny about Chloe's situation.'

I agreed that she had, but I could hardly believe that she'd found it out just by looking at some cards. How *could* she have?

On Thursday I stayed at school late because I had to finish off an art project. Sophie was doing something in the art room too, but we hadn't spoken to each other. When our tutor left, though, and we started clearing up, she came over to me.

I felt a bit nervous because she'd snubbed me all week, and seeing as she'd fetched Zara a real slap around the face I thought she might be about to do the same to me. It's nothing to do with me, I was going to say. It's not me who's psychic.

She emptied a bowl of paste into the sink and

started washing it down. 'About me and Sky . . .' she said.

'What?' I asked nervously.

'I don't know how your friend Zara operates or what she's on, but I don't believe she's psychic. Psychic!' She shook her head. 'That's just a load of rubbish.'

I didn't know what to say. Zara and I had made up the scam with the star signs, and the psychometric stuff had been a trick too, so on the one hand it *was* rubbish. But on the other hand, she'd got so many things right since. So many big things . . .

'It *is* rubbish, isn't it?' she repeated. 'You must know it is.'

'She found out about Chloe's brother, though,' I said. 'And how did she know about you and Anton?'

Sophie swished water around the sink. 'I wonder.'

'It is true, then?' I asked daringly.

'Well, it's definitely true that I fancied him. And true that I went to meet him without Sky being there. But that's all, though if you listen to Zara you'd think the two of us were on the verge of running away together.'

I didn't say anything.

'Zara blew it out of all proportion. She somehow

knew I fancied him – I suppose that wasn't difficult – and played on it. And I met him once but that's all it was. I wasn't going to take it any further.'

I pretended to be busy washing up my palette, feeling embarrassed at having her confessing to me. 'Why are you telling me? D'you want me to tell Sky what you've said?'

She shook her head. 'No point. Everyone knows now and it's more or less pushed me and Anton together.'

I stared at her.

'Well, everyone thought Anton and I were an item, so *we* thought we might just as well go along with it. Be hung for a sheep as well as a lamb, or whatever the saying is.'

'So . . .'

'So, forget us. I'm just concerned about you and your friend making more trouble, interfering where you shouldn't. What's she going to do next?'

I shrugged. 'I don't know.'

'Someone told me you're holding a seance. That's dangerous, all that stuff.'

'It's not *me* doing it.'

'Course it is. You're in it together, aren't you? A right couple of little witches,' she said bitterly.

'But I don't really want to do any more!' I blurted out, and I would have liked to have told her that Zara had upset me, too, by telling me that my dad had a secret. A secret that I never stopped wondering about . . .

'Well, don't, then,' she said. 'You don't have to. You've got a mind of your own, haven't you?'

'But she's my best friend.'

'Best friend!' She shrugged. 'Yeah, I used to have one of those.'

Chapter Ten

'I don't know what the matter is with this class lately,' Miss Robbins said a few days later. 'All the animation seems to have gone out of you.'

'What's that mean?' someone asked.

'What I mean is, you're all looking rather wary – as if you're walking on eggshells. You look like that when you've got a test coming up – but there aren't any more tests.'

'Hurray,' someone said.

'Of course I can see that something's been happening as far as your seating arrangements are concerned,' Miss Robbins went on, 'and girls who've been sitting next to each other for years are no longer doing so.' She looked at us carefully, her eyes moving across the class. 'I don't know what's caused all this and I don't want to know, but I'd certainly rather have you all back the way you were, silly and annoying as that sometimes was.'

No one said anything. Miss Robbins was right, though, and obviously had more insight than I thought. Generally, the class was no longer a happy one. We never had giggling fits or gossip sessions, or got together to do impromptu impersonations of teachers in the way we'd done before. And as well as Sky and Sophie not speaking (which in turn made a difference to Poppy and Lois), Chloe and India weren't speaking to each other either because Chloe was convinced that, because she'd only confided in India about her brother, it had to have been her who'd told Zara.

I felt the walking on eggshells thing too, waiting to see if Zara was going to come up with anything else about my dad; both anticipating it and dreading it. I wanted to know, yet I didn't.

But a few more days went by and she didn't say another word about him – in fact she was really friendly and back to her old self – and I wondered if she might have just said both those things for effect and perhaps wished she hadn't. I was a bit restrained with her, though, for all sorts of reasons I didn't feel as best-friendly as I used to, so I think it was to try and get back in with me again she offered to do me a proper Tarot reading. At first I refused, scared that it was just an excuse to bring up something about my dad, but she kept telling me it was a love spread she was going to do, and that she'd had really positive vibes about me and the boy I'd seen – about Lofty. In the end (after seeing him again and getting another smile) I was so keen to know whether anything was going to happen between us that I decided to let her do it. As she said, if your best friend is psychic then you'd be mad not to take advantage of that.

The seance to contact Lois's mum had been put off a while – until the night of the next full moon – so Zara arranged to come over and do a reading for me on Thursday evening, a day when we never got much homework.

The night before that, I thought I'd have a word with Dad; I wanted to make sure that if they bumped into each other on the stairs he wouldn't say anything to upset her. If he didn't provoke her, then maybe she wouldn't say anything nasty about him.

'Zara's coming over tomorrow,' I started, 'and I don't want you to say anything horrible to her.'

'Well, I won't say anything at all, then! That's easiest.'

'You know what I mean, Dad. Can't you just be nice to her?'

He groaned. 'Does she have to come here?'

I tried to keep my temper. 'She's not hurting you, is she? And . . . and she's having such a rough time at home,' I added, thinking that I'd try and make him feel a bit sorry for her. 'Her mum's awful . . .'

'Awfully drunk!'

'She just drinks all the time now,' I elaborated.

'Terrible . . .' Dad tutted.

'And I do feel –'

Here he interrupted me and I nearly lost it with him. '*Feel!*' he said. '*Feel* with two "e"s and no "w". *Feel!*'

I bit back a swearword. 'I do *feel* really sorry for Zara,' I said through gritted teeth. 'She told me she likes coming here because we're such a nice family,' I lied, and it was a good job Mum wasn't around because she would have seen through that one straightaway. Dad didn't, though. Instead he looked rather pleased with himself.

'Oh,' he said, nodding. 'Does she?'

'Yes, so it's good for her to come here and see how an ordinary family lives, isn't it? Otherwise she wouldn't know.'

He grunted, but he looked quite smug. I thought he'd be OK.

The next evening – well, it all started off well. When Zara arrived I was making earrings ready to give as Christmas presents, and she helped me with the finishing touches by brushing silver leaf, which is very, very fragile, on to some crescent moon shapes and fixing them on to wires. Really pretty, they looked.

I was going to put silver wire hooks on them next but found I'd mislaid the little packet of them that I'd bought. Annoyed with myself, I rushed up and down stairs a bit without finding them, then Zara said that she'd try and dowse for them.

'Go on, then!' I said, cross with myself for not putting them away with all my other earring bits.

She took a large sheet of paper and did a rough plan of the house: downstairs with sitting room, dining room and kitchen, and upstairs with two bedrooms and study. Then she held her dowsing crystal over each room in turn and asked whether my hooks were in this particular room, yes or no. It swung around, saying no to each, so then she tried upstairs and it said yes to my bedroom, which was, of course, the obvious place anyway. She tried to narrow this down by making another plan, this time of the room with bed, wardrobe, desk, table, bookcase in place. She dowsed over each one in turn, and the crystal said no to each of these except *bed*, so we pulled it right out and had a good look under there with a torch. It all took ages and we didn't find a thing, so by the time we started the Tarot spread I was in a negative sort of mood and ready not to believe in it. The fact that all that dowsing had failed didn't seem to worry Zara much. She just said she felt they *were* there somewhere and would eventually turn up of their own accord.

She unwrapped the cards and placed them on the table.

'I'm going to do you a look-see spread,' she said. 'You can ask a question about this guy and see what the Tarot has to say about him.'

We did the cleansing bell business, and then she dipped her head down to the table as if she was bowing to the cards, and then she did the centring to call down the light into herself. Part of me always wanted to giggle when she did this, and the *earthing*, but I didn't. Because she was at my house I was very careful not to do anything to make her cross.

I shuffled the cards, then gave them back to her and she, very solemnly, cut them into three piles. She collected the piles up again, then laid out seven cards, face up, in a pattern: three in a semi-circle around the top, three at the bottom and the last card in the centre.

'What do you want to ask?' she said then.

'You know!'

'You've got to ask formally.'

'OK,' I said, feeling a bit daft. 'I want to know if the boy I'm thinking of – the one I call Lofty – is at all interested in me.'

She nodded her head, ran her hands over the cards like she was getting some sort of warmth from them, then she started saying what each one stood for. The first two cards stood for present circumstances and possibilities, then came past actions, future actions and so on. The final one in the middle stood for out-come.

I must say, even though I wasn't a true believer, that what she did say made an awful lot of sense. The present circumstances – well, I hadn't told her that each time I'd seen him it had been raining, but she said something about bad weather being lucky for bumping into him. She also said that I was influenced in my feelings by something I'd found attractive in a previous boyfriend, and that was true too, because the boy I'd met on holiday had had the same little gap between his front teeth, which I'd found really sexy.

There were quite a few things like this that she got right; things that rang true. It was all quite uncanny, really, and more than made up for the dowsing that hadn't worked.

The last card, the outcome one, was a man helping a woman off a horse. She said this was good and meant that we'd form a close relationship in the future. She then asked me to pick a final card from the deck and place it on top of the last card. This, she said, would emphasise the outcome. It was of a man holding a golden goblet.

'This is you,' she said.

'How can it be me?' I said. 'It's a man.'

'That doesn't make any difference. It's someone holding up the cup of plenty, just about to drink from it.'

'Is that good?'

She nodded. 'It's excellent.'

'So . . . next time I see him – Lofty – shall I go straight over and start chatting him up?'

She nodded again. 'Yes. Do it. I can definitely see a future for the two of you.'

She did the *earthing* business, then collected up the cards, put them in their pack and didn't speak any more about anything psychic. We put on a couple of CDs and by the time I thought to look at my watch it was quite late.

'Nearly ten-thirty. You'd better go now before the pubs turn out,' I said.

She looked at me sharply. 'What d'you mean by that? You having a go?'

I shook my head vigorously, feeling myself go red. She'd obviously thought I was talking about her mum. 'I didn't mean anything . . . just that you get blokes hanging about outside the Lamb and Flag on the corner and it's not very nice going past it.' I hesitated. 'D'you want to ring your mum to let her know you're on your way?'

She looked at me and frowned. 'No thanks,' she said, and I thought I'd probably put my foot in it again: her mum was bound to be out drinking – and even if she wasn't I bet they hadn't had their telephone reconnected.

We went downstairs. Mum was in the kitchen and called hello and goodbye, and then Dad came out of the sitting room. Of course, the first thing he hit upon was the new piercing on Zara's eyebrow. This had a small gold bar in it, but at least wasn't red any more.

'Hello! New eyebrow jewellery?' he asked.

She nodded at him coolly.

'Where's the next piercing, then?' he said, then added quickly, 'No, you'd better not tell me. It's bound to be somewhere rude!'

'Yes, never mind that, Dad,' I said, beginning to feel hot, and I started to usher Zara out of the door before he said anything else.

'Goodnight, then. Mind how you go,' Dad said, quite nicely, and as he spoke he put out a hand and patted her on the shoulder in what I thought was a friendly sort of way. The moment he touched her, though, she flinched. Not because his touch had surprised her, but in the way that you'd flinch if the dirtiest, smelliest beggar in the street came up to you and put his arm on you. As if you were revolted.

Well, I was *so* embarrassed. He, luckily, didn't appear to have noticed – or pretended he hadn't noticed. Funny, I wouldn't normally have been on his side but he really hadn't done anything to deserve that. OK, he'd been his usual crass self, but no worse than usual, and actually quite a bit better. He'd smiled at her. He'd talked to her quite reasonably. He'd wished her goodnight. So why had she flinched like that when he'd touched her?

I couldn't bring myself to ask her. I just waved until she'd disappeared out of sight and went upstairs.

The thing that troubled me was that it really looked as if her reaction had been unconscious. She hadn't done it deliberately to be nasty, she'd done it without thinking. It had been an automatic reaction to being touched by someone she found obnoxious and hateful. Why, though? Why my dad? What had he done?

As I tried to sleep with all these thoughts going through my head I was glad about one thing: that she'd been wrong about the dowsing business. The little package I'd lost hadn't been under the bed, so she wasn't right about everything. Perhaps she was wrong about my dad as well.

But then . . . just as I was drifting off, I flung my hand out of bed so that it rested on a folded-back throw and felt a tiny plastic bag. I sat up, put the light on and discovered the packet we'd been looking for – one of the little hooks had poked out of the top and somehow attached itself to my throw. It hadn't been *under* the bed, it had been *on* the bed.

So she'd been right about that, as well.

Chapter Eleven

Friday night, full moon, the night of the seance, and five girls were kneeling at a table in my room. The girls were me, Zara, Lois, Sky and Poppy, and the room was lit by candles and was suitably eerie-looking.

I hadn't *wanted* it to be at my house, but for one reason or another we'd ended up there. Holding it at Zara's, of course, was out of the question with her mother being the way she was (Zara had made the excuse that she had the flu) and although Lois's house would have been the first choice seeing as it was her mum we were trying to contact, she said her dad would have gone absolutely mad if he'd found out what she was up to. Poppy had to share a bedroom, so she was no good, and Sky's little sister was having a sleepover that night and would be bound to come bursting in right in the middle of the proceedings.

Seeing as my mum and dad were going to be out until quite late at some dinner with Dad's firm, then my house it had to be. I'd told them I had friends coming round and they hadn't asked what we were going to do – I think they were just really pleased that I'd said 'friends' in the plural.

I didn't know whether Zara minded about it being at mine – she hadn't said. And when I'd asked her, she made out that she hadn't flinched at my dad's touch last time when she'd come over. 'It was nothing,' she'd said. 'I just shivered, that's all.'

'It was more than that,' I'd insisted.

'Well, someone must have walked over my grave!' she'd said, and she pulled a weird face and rolled her eyes back in her head, which didn't exactly make me feel better.

She'd arrived first that evening, bringing two big purple candles, some black muslin to drape over the curtains and some incense sticks to burn – it would all add to the atmosphere, she said. I knew, of course, that she'd been looking forward to this for ages; it was her big occasion, her chance to prove what she could do, show how very psychic she was.

I'd borrowed the coffee table from downstairs so we could kneel around it and Zara had written the letters of the alphabet on cut-up pieces of paper, with two extra squares saying YES and NO. These were all arranged in a circle on the table with a wine glass standing in the centre. Lois had also brought along a photo of her mum, which was supposedly going to encourage her spirit to make herself known to us.

Looking around and seeing the five of us kneeling around the table whispering nervously to each other, the whole place flickering with candlelight and the smoke from the incense sticks hanging in swirls around the ceiling, it didn't seem like my bedroom at all, but a strange and mystic place which could have been anywhere, at any time. I couldn't say I was enjoying it, though. It was all a bit *too* mystical for me.

Zara got out four crystals and placed one on each corner of the table. 'These are protective crystals,' she said. 'They'll act as a shield from any negative influences.'

Sky nodded. 'I know something about those,' she said. 'My mum's got an amethyst she says is protective.'

I felt for the tiger's eye in my pocket and touched it for luck. I usually kept it on me, although I didn't really know if I believed it had any powers.

'Zara . . . are you really sure it's OK to do this?' Poppy asked, glancing over to Lois, who was looking pale and worried on the other side of the table. 'Only I had a book about magic and stuff and it said that you shouldn't try to invoke the dead unless you're very experienced.'

'How d'you know I'm not?' Zara asked.

Poppy shrugged.

'Well, you can't be *that* experienced, can you?' Sky said, but nicely. 'I mean, the first we even knew you were psychic was a couple of months back.'

'And then suddenly you'd turned into Mystic Meg!' Poppy added, laughing a little.

Zara didn't laugh. 'Don't start being negative,' she said. 'Or it *will* all go wrong. The last thing we want is negative vibes.'

We all immediately went quiet. What would happen if it 'all went wrong'? I wondered. Did that just mean that no spirits would arrive? That we wouldn't be able to contact Lois's mum? Or did it mean (as in a book I'd once read) that the powers of evil would be invoked and a wicked elemental would appear and do all sorts of devious things?

Zara suddenly turned and looked at me sharply, and I wondered with a shock if she'd actually read my thoughts.

No! I quickly told myself. No, of course she hadn't. She wasn't *that* good. I was letting my imagination run away with me.

Poppy was sitting next to me and she gave me a half-smile. 'You OK?' she whispered. 'You look as if you've seen a ghost.'

'I just hope I don't!' I whispered back.

Zara frowned at me. 'Please cleanse the room, Ella,' she said, handing me the bell, and I got up and shook the bell around the perimeter, as I always did.

As I sat down again, Zara got to her feet. She stretched out her arms and said, 'And now I call on four archangels to stand in each corner!'

It was a real shock when she said this, frightening and hysterical at the same time, and I was scared to look at the others in case I started giggling.

'Michael, the Archangel of the Sun, Gabriel, Raphael and Zadkiel!' she went on, and I thought to myself, she fancies herself, doesn't she – asking for four archangels to come to hang around my bedroom with a group of schoolgirls. As if they didn't have anything better to do! I was trying to think things like this, treat the whole business lightly, but really I was absolutely terrified. If she actually conjured anything up and I saw a dead person, I thought I'd absolutely die of fright.

Zara didn't seem to see anything outrageous in what she was doing, but was as calm as if she invoked archangels every day of the week. She sat down and put her finger on the upturned wine glass. 'And may my personal guide be with me in this quest,' she added, bowing her head as if she was saying her prayers.

A moment passed, and then she looked around the circle. I couldn't meet her eyes because I felt squirmy with embarrassment. 'I want you all to put your fingers on the wine glass,' she said. 'Just the tips of your fingers . . . touch it very lightly.'

We all did this.

Zara breathed in deeply and then out in a rush, making the smoke spirals from the incense sticks shiver and curl. 'Is there anybody there?' she asked momentously.

We were all holding our breath, watching the glass, and I thought to myself, *what if it went to NO?* How mad would that be?

It didn't move at all, though.

'Spirits of the upper air . . . we invite you to our table!' Zara said. 'Is there anybody there?'

Suddenly – suddenly – the glass gave a lurch to

one side. We all looked at each other, startled.

'Wow!' Poppy breathed.

Zara frowned at her. 'Concentrate on the glass,' she said.

We did. At least, intrigued as to what was going to happen next, I certainly did.

'Is there anybody there?' Zara said yet again, and the glass moved to the right in a jerky movement, then reversed itself and moved smoothly to the piece of paper saying YES.

We all gave little cries of excitement, although I didn't quite know how I felt at that stage. Did I believe it? Did I really believe a spirit was there? No, of course I didn't. I thought someone – Zara, probably – must be pushing the glass to where she wanted it to go. And yet . . .

'What is your name?' Zara asked.

The glass began moving again, going round and round in the middle for a while before lurching over to the 'V' and then touching briefly on the letters I O L E T in turn.

'Violet!' we all said.

Zara looked round the circle. 'Did anyone have an Auntie Violet who has now passed away? Or a granny called Violet?'

No one had.

'No matter,' Zara said. She closed her eyes. 'I can feel your presence, Violet. Thank you for joining us.'

Poppy glanced at me and raised her eyebrows slightly, signifying disbelief. I was reassured. It was just a game, of course it was. Zara was showing off a bit, mucking about.

'Can we ask how long she's been dead?' Sky asked.

'Please tell us in what year you died,' Zara said, and then realised that she hadn't put any numbers around the circle. She changed the question to, 'Who was on the throne when you died?'

'Violet' didn't seem to want to answer this. The glass started off going to V and we all thought it was going to spell VICTORIA, but instead it moved around a mish-mash of random letters which didn't mean a thing.

'We seek to contact someone on the other side,' Zara said, giving up on the previous question.

I glanced across at Lois, who looked scared half to death.

'It is the mother of someone here present,' Zara added, nodding at Lois to speak, while I wondered to myself why, when you were addressing spirits, you had to be so formal.

'Hello? Hello, Mum,' Lois said in a frightened whisper. 'Are you there?'

'If there is a message for Lois, please speak through the glass,' Zara instructed the empty air above her head, where the spirits presumably were.

The wine glass circled round a few times, then moved to the B. After that, with us all making big eyes at each other, it quickly became obvious what it was going to say. It spelled out the letters for BE HAPPY LOIS more or less without a pause.

Lois smiled, well pleased with this. 'That's nice. And are you happy, Mum?' she asked.

The glass was moving well now. It answered, WE ARE OF THE WIND, which didn't make much sense to us, although Zara nodded and said she understood. 'People on the other side are not like us,' she said to Lois. 'Not happy or unhappy. They're sort of ethereal.'

Lois nodded, intent on the glass. 'Is there anything else, Mum?' she asked.

The glass started moving again and although my arm was aching a bit, I tried to keep my touch on it loose. I didn't think I was pushing it round, though once you kind of knew what it was going to say, it was difficult to stop *thinking* it towards those letters. GO

TOWARDS THE LIGHT, it spelled out, and everyone was very impressed by this.

I wasn't so much, though, because I knew one of the books which Zara had borrowed from the library had been called *Going Towards the Light* and it just seemed too much of a coincidence. 'Are you sure you're not pushing the glass?' I asked Zara, but she gave me such a furious look that I wished I hadn't spoken.

'Do you have a message for my dad?' Lois asked next, but then the glass went a bit haywire and started whizzing backwards and forwards like no one's business, not spelling anything that made sense.

'I expect some mischievous spirit has come up,' Zara said. 'That does sometimes happen.'

'Has my mum gone now, then?' Lois asked, disappointed. 'There were some other things I wanted to ask her.'

Zara nodded. 'They never stay long.' She addressed the glass. 'Is Violet there again now?'

The glass shot to NO.

'Who is speaking, then?'

I HAVE NO NAME.

Zara said, 'Have you a message for anyone here?'

YES.

'Who is the message for?'

The glass hesitated for a moment, and then swung towards E. As soon as it did this I began to feel apprehensive. It was going to be a message for me; I knew it was. But I didn't *want* a message. Why couldn't it speak to one of the others? I tried to make my finger on the glass a little more resistant, so that it wouldn't go to the rest of the letters in my name, but that didn't work and of course it went on to the letters L L A.

Zara nodded to me. 'Ella. Ask what the message is.'

'What is the message?' I asked dutifully, and the minute I said that the glass seemed to go *mad*. While I watched, horrified, willing it not to, it went straight to the letters K I L L one after the other, shooting across the table as if it was demented.

It paused, then went to the letters E and R. KILLER.

'Killer,' Zara said in a strange voice. 'Who is a killer? Is it Ella?'

'Of course I'm not a killer!' I said, and Poppy gave a high-pitched giggle.

We all still had our fingers on the glass and it started moving again. HIM, it said.

Zara looked at me and silently mouthed, 'Your dad.'

'No!' I said.

Zara addressed the glass. 'How did he kill?' she said.

I gave a cry of protest – I didn't want to hear any more – and the glass whizzed across the table, making those on the other side of it stretch out their arms to the full. It then kind of skidded to a stop, overturned and crashed on to the floor, where it broke.

I stared around, feeling sick and shaky, as if I'd been punched in the stomach.

There was a long silence when all we could hear was the candles, puttering and flickering. 'What did *that* all mean?' Poppy said eventually.

'Wasn't that weird . . .' Sky said shakily.

There was another moment's silence. 'Ladies,' Zara said then, rather grandly, 'the seance is over.'

Chapter Twelve

I'd seen the others out – shaken and quiet, they'd hardly said goodbye – and then, not wanting to go back upstairs, had gone into the sitting room. Zara had come down a few moments later and, without saying anything about what had happened, sat on the sofa and put the TV on. There was some pop star competition on and she was watching it while I just stared at the screen, still shaking.

Killer. Killer. Killer.

The word went through my head. Why had it said that? It didn't really mean that, surely? Not that he'd actually *killed* someone. Not my dad . . .

'Wow! Look at him!' Zara said, as a blond guy came on the TV and started chatting to the judges. 'He ought to win on looks alone.'

I looked, but couldn't see him.

Killer.

How could she just sit there, pretending nothing had happened? Pretending that she hadn't just said what she had?

I waited until another face appeared on the TV screen. 'It's not really true about my dad, is it?' I said, and my breath was all fluttery in my throat and I could hear my heartbeat thudding through my ears. 'You didn't mean it.'

'What?' She frowned at me, looking annoyed at being distracted from the screen. 'I dunno.'

'But you can't just say something like that . . .'

'It wasn't *me* who said it.'

'Well, it was sort of you, wasn't it?'

'I'm just the medium.'

'Yeah, right.'

She looked at me with her head on one side. 'And you know what they say,' she added, sounding so cocky and smug that I almost hated her. 'Don't shoot the messenger!'

I searched my mind for what I could say to get through to her. 'Look,' I said desperately. 'You can't just leave it like this. I've got to know more.'

She was staring at the TV screen now, watching the blond guy. 'You saw what happened when I tried to ask the spirit something else – everything went mad. And quite honestly, I don't want to talk about it any more. The spirits don't like people questioning what they say. You just have to try and take it on board.'

'What – you tell me my dad's a killer and I just have to live with that?'

She shrugged.

'He *can't* be. He's just an ordinary bloke.'

'I bet murderers' families always say that,' she said, and I really did hate her then. 'I mean, I told you ages ago that there was something strange . . . that he had some dark secret, didn't I?'

'Yeah, but I thought you meant he was a gambler or drinker or something. Nothing like *that*. That he'd . . . he'd . . .'

While I was struggling with the words, she was watching the screen where the blond guy was dancing. She suddenly clapped her hands. 'Look at him! Talk about fit!'

'I mean, my dad's really *nice*,' I said, and my eyes suddenly filled with tears, thinking of times when he'd been nice, or thoughtful, or kind. I knew he was a silly old buffer sometimes, but mainly, *mostly*, he was OK. And he certainly wasn't, couldn't be . . .

'He's not always nice,' she said sharply. 'He's had a

few digs at me over the years. Always having goes at me, he is.'

'Yeah, but he doesn't *mean* it,' I said uneasily. 'Half the time he just thinks he's being funny.'

'Oh. Ha ha. Remind me to laugh,' she said bitterly. 'D'you remember last Christmas? I came round one afternoon and he wouldn't let me in! He said you had relatives round and that Christmas was a family time.'

I felt myself flushing. She'd come round on Boxing Day. Boxing Day! We'd been having tea and Dad wouldn't let her in. 'It wasn't anything about you, it was just that my gran was here and she's a bit dippy.'

'No, it wasn't *that*, it was because he thought I might spoil your lovely little family gathering,' she said. 'You and your brother, your mum and dad and dear old granny. The perfect family!'

'No families are perfect –' I began, but she cut across me.

'Oh, don't give me any of that crap. You don't know anything about other people's families.'

She went back to staring at the screen and I didn't speak for ages, thinking to myself that I wished – really wished – we hadn't ever started anything. I was also thinking that Zara had changed. In fact, *everything* had changed: the things we did, the other girls, life in general . . . nothing was as nice as it had been, even though we were now that very thing we'd strived to be: *popular*.

And what was going to happen now? How could I carry on being best friends with the girl who'd practically accused my dad of being a murderer? What were the other girls going to say to me about it on Monday? And had there really been some sort of message from the other side, or had she just made everything up?

'Are you *really* psychic?' I asked desperately.

'Of course I am. What more proof d'you need?'

'But at the beginning you said you weren't.'

'That was just because I didn't want to scare you off. I thought you'd be too much of a wimp to do stuff otherwise.'

'So if you are, why can't you find out anything else? Why can't you tell me the whole story about my dad?'

She didn't say anything.

'I don't believe you!' I said suddenly. It was all I had, really. My last defence. 'I don't believe you're really psychic.'

'What?' she said irritably.

'I think you've made up the whole thing. You're

just having a laugh.'

She glanced at me. 'If that's what you want to believe,' she said carelessly. 'If it's easier for you to believe that – OK.'

'You said you were going to *pretend* to be psychic, and that's what you've done.'

'OK, Miss Knowall, how could I have made all that up?' she said. 'There's no way that anyone could have found out all the things that I have.'

I shook my head. 'I don't know how, but I'm not going to believe you ever again.'

She didn't say anything and I felt desperate to provoke a reaction from her. How could she just sit there as if nothing had happened?

'I'm not going to believe anything else that you say – and I don't want to be your friend any more!'

'OK, then,' she said, and she stood up. I thought she was leaving but she went towards the patio window instead. 'I'll tell you all about your dad, shall I? I'll show you.'

I shrank back from her, horrified.

'We have to go outside for that,' she said, nodding towards the windows on to the garden. 'Outside to where he buried the body.'

'No!'

'Yes,' she said. 'Your dad put her in the garden.'

I stared at her speechlessly. It was like being in a dream. We'd just been messing around and suddenly it had all gone wrong. Horribly, wickedly wrong.

She drew the curtains open and slid the glass door across. As I got up from the sofa a blast of wind from outside caught me and made me shiver, but it was a fresh kind of cold . . . not like the frightening, sickening shivers running through my body.

'Whereabouts are we going?' I stammered.

She didn't reply, just stepped through the windows and out on to the patio. I followed her, thinking – a bit hysterically – of the soaps. On TV people were being buried under patios on a regular basis.

Not in real life, though.

Not *really*.

She crossed the patio with only the light from the full moon to see by and I followed her on to the lawn. Further down the garden we passed our garden furniture, wrapped in plastic sheeting for the winter and forming strange, surreal shapes, and then came to the flower beds and the shed. Beyond this were the dark fir trees of the wood, swaying now in the wind, stretching back into the darkness.

'Where are you going?'

She stopped. 'I'm not *quite* sure. She's around here somewhere, though.' She shot a look at me. 'The person your dad buried is here.'

I tugged at her arm. 'No, she's not!' I cried. 'Stop it!'

She shrugged, her face impassive in the moonlight. 'You said you wanted to know.'

I started crying. She didn't react, and when I looked at her she had her eyes shut.

'Someone's near,' she said. 'I feel a spirit presence very close.'

I couldn't say anything, just kept crying.

'Someone from the spirit world is with us,' she said, holding her arms up to the sky. 'He buried her here under the trees . . .'

'No!' I sobbed.

'She's close by . . . very close. Shut your eyes, Ella. You can feel her near us, can't you? Her spirit is walking by . . . her shadow is touching us.' She sounded as if she was in a trance now, far away. 'I hear her voice calling to us from the other side . . .'

'No, there's nothing here! Nothing! You're making it all up!' I felt that if I could deny it, deny it all along the way, then it wouldn't be true.

Zara was mad. She had to be.

Because if she wasn't mad . . .

'If we stay here until midnight we'll see her!' Zara said. She began to laugh. 'The witching hour of midnight when the graves give up their dead . . .'

As I stared at her, horrified, I heard a car pulling up on our gravel drive. Mum and Dad were back from their dinner.

The change in Zara was instantaneous. She became brisk, matter-of-fact. 'Well, here they are and you can ask your dad yourself. Ask him about the body in the woods,' she said, beginning to walk away.

'No!' I tried to grab hold of her arm. 'You're not going!'

She began to run across the garden but I was after her, calling her to stop. She ran up the garden and tried to get out of the side gate and on to the road, but I was with her all the way, hanging on to her, telling her she had to come back and face my dad; tell him what she'd told me.

As we struggled by the side gate, Mum must have come through the house and seen the windows open. I saw her appear on the patio, straining to see what was going on outside.

'Ella!' she called. 'Is that you? What are you doing out there?'

I gripped Zara's arm more tightly. 'You're not going!' I said between gritted teeth.

'Let go of me!' Zara wriggled and squirmed to get her arm away but there was no way I was letting go. She was taller than me, and a bit heftier, but she wasn't getting away.

'What are you *doing*?' Mum called again.

Heaving, I pulled Zara closer to the house.

'Is that Zara with you?' Mum asked. 'Whatever's going on?'

Zara suddenly went limp and unresistant. Maybe she'd realised that I wasn't going to let her get away. She allowed herself to be led into the sitting room where Mum stood wearing her best black dress with high heels and dangling earrings. She frowned at the mud on our shoes.

'What *is* it?' she said. 'What on earth have you two been doing out there in the cold?'

'Wait,' I said, puffing, and I pointed towards the front door to indicate that we'd wait for Dad, who could be heard putting the car in the garage. 'Wait a minute.'

'You're getting mud all over the carpet,' Mum said, and I just stared at her. As if that sort of thing mattered now.

It seemed to take for ever for Dad to come into the room, and when he did he just looked at us grouped in front of him like some sort of tableau, and stopped dead.

'What's all this about?'

'Zara's got something to say to you,' I said.

'I haven't,' Zara said, very composed. 'I haven't got anything to say. This is your problem, not mine.'

There was a moment's silence. Just a tiny moment, but it felt to me that everything was balanced and waiting. I could have laughed then, said it was nothing and lived with it, or I could have gone on.

And I went on.

'Zara said . . . Zara told me that you'd killed someone, Dad.'

Dad's face showed horror, then disbelief and amazement.

'She told me that you'd killed someone and put them in the garden.'

'No!' Mum cried. 'What a wicked thing to say. Why ever should she make up something like that?'

Dad walked over to Zara and, gripping her arm, turned her round to face him.

'Ow!' she said. 'Let me go.'

'Not until we've cleared this up. This is not only

ridiculous but also a very serious accusation.'

Zara compressed her lips and Dad shook her arm as if to make her talk. Eventually she said, 'It was just for a laugh.'

'And one which I don't find at all funny,' he said. 'Would you like to come down to the police station and repeat it?'

'I was just . . . just messing around,' she said. 'Can't you take a joke?'

'A *joke*?' Mum asked. She appealed to me. 'Why would she say something like that?'

I hesitated. 'She . . . we had a seance – you know, sitting round in a circle with your fingers on a glass. It said some stuff to the other girls, and then it said that Dad was a killer.' I glanced at Zara, who actually looked as if she was bored by the whole thing. 'And then we went out into the garden and she said you'd buried someone out there in the woods and their spirit was nearby.'

Mum gave a little scream, open-mouthed, gasping, and when I looked at Dad he'd gone white.

It was then that I felt *really* scared. 'What?!' I asked, beginning to tremble. 'Is . . . is it true, then?'

Mum gave a long drawn-out gasp. She came across and put her arm around me, and I knew that above my head she and Dad were mouthing words to each other.

'*Is it true?*' I asked again, more fearfully, because if it wasn't, then why weren't they laughing and saying that they'd never heard anything so stupid in all their lives?

'We should have told her,' Mum said to Dad in a whisper.

I gave a little cry and suddenly felt all swimmy in the head. I've never fainted in my life but I thought I was about to then.

Mum led me to the sofa, sat me down and began rubbing at my hands. 'We should have told you,' I heard her say through the swimminess. 'I know we should have told you. It was just that the time never seemed right.'

'And you couldn't talk about it,' Dad said to her in a low voice.

'No, I couldn't,' Mum agreed.

'Tell me now,' I said fearfully. '*Is* there someone buried in the woods?'

Zara wrenched herself away from Dad and he grabbed hold of her again. 'You're staying,' he said. 'You can't just say something like this and then run away.'

'*Just tell me!*' I said desperately to Mum, because I

175

was so *so* scared.

'Darling, it's quite simple,' Mum said. 'As soon as Zara said something about being buried in the woods I realised what this was all about . . .'

'*What?*' I said urgently.

'Well, you know there's a big gap between you and your brother?'

I nodded.

'There was another baby in between. A baby who died.'

'There would have been three of you,' Dad put in.

'And you *killed* it?' I asked fearfully.

Dad looked at me and sighed. 'Ella,' he said. 'Do you really believe I'm a child murderer?'

'The baby was stillborn,' Mum said, and she was crying a little. 'It was a girl and she went to eight months, but she died.'

I swallowed. 'What was her name?'

'We didn't name her,' Dad said. 'We thought that would make her more real.'

'And we didn't want to have a funeral or anything so we just brought her home with us.'

I was silent, taking all this in. Dad looked out of the window. 'She's buried in the woods,' he said. 'There's a woodland burial ground over the back –

you probably didn't know that.'

'So she's quite close to us; just under the trees,' Mum said.

I looked at Zara. 'That's what she said – under the trees.'

No one spoke for a while; the only sound was of Mum giving little gaspy sobs.

'OK, then,' Dad said to Zara eventually. 'What do you know, how do you know it – and what was the idea of doing all this?'

She shrugged. 'I was just having a laugh! God, some people really get their knickers in a twist, don't they?' This was such a gross thing to say that no one bothered to respond to it. She went on, 'I was pretending to be psychic, that's all. Giving everyone a bit of excitement in their lives.'

'*Pretending?*' I asked.

'Of course she was pretending,' Dad said. 'But why don't we call it *lying*, because that's what it was.'

'But how could you find out all that stuff about everyone?' I asked Zara.

She shrugged. 'By using my eyes and my ears, that's how.'

'What about Sophie and Anton?'

'I saw them out together! Easy.'

'And Lois's mum – all that stuff about the flowers by the photo?'

'The photo of her mum is on the table in her front room, Dumbo. You can see it from the street.'

'So all that tonight, with the glass . . . were you pushing it round?'

'Sometimes,' she said. 'But then once everyone got an inkling of where it might go, they pushed it there themselves.'

I opened and closed my mouth, thoughts hammering through my head. 'But all that other stuff. What about Chloe?'

'Her brother's case was reported in the paper,' she said. 'The case was there in the small print for anyone to see. It was obvious that that was why they didn't go abroad to live.'

'But what about *this*, tonight?'

'Yes. How did you know about our baby?' Dad asked.

Zara pursed her lips and looked away.

Dad said. 'Well, we can wait. All night if needs be.'

'Or we can go to the police . . .' Mum said.

There was a long silence. 'All right,' Zara said after some moments. 'I'll tell you how I knew – my mum used to be a nurse on a maternity ward.'

Mum gasped. 'At St Luke's?' she asked.

Zara nodded. 'When we met you out shopping, she recognised you and told me that you'd lost a baby. When I asked her what happened when babies died, she told me what you'd done.'

'How dare she!' Mum said. 'She had no business doing that. That's confidential information.'

Zara shrugged and I just sat there, stunned, trying to sort things out in my head. All the stuff she'd said, all of it, just found-out stuff. She wasn't psychic at all. Just clever. Very clever and very devious.

'So, I can go now, can I?' Zara said, moving away from Dad.

'Do what you like,' Dad said. 'I don't want to see you round here again.'

She went out of the room and they didn't even look at her. I went after her because there was something I really wanted to know.

'Why did you do all this?' I asked.

She compressed her lips again, staring at me.

'I thought it was just to make ourselves popular,' I persisted. 'Why did you turn on me and try and ruin my life? You've got to tell me!'

'Oh, have I?' she said.

I nodded.

'Well, how about because you're so bloody smug with your big house and your perfect family and your patronising ways! I can see the way you look down on me and my mum! "*Shall we go to my house because your mum's drunk?*"' she said in an imitation of my voice. 'Make sure everyone knows, why don't you?'

I stared at her.

'And what about when you were out with your brother and hid so you wouldn't have to say hello? Ashamed of me, were you?' she demanded. 'You'd rather be with the others than be friends with me, wouldn't you? Admit it!'

Of *course* I would, I felt like saying, but I didn't speak.

'I wanted to show you what it was like to have a real problem in your life. Give you something else to think about. Besides,' she added, 'I just wanted to see if I could get away with it. Your dad was horrible to me; it was something to do.'

It was something to do. All the pain she'd caused, just for something to do.

I stared at her and all the stuffing seemed to go out of me, leaving me tired, confused and miserable. I just couldn't think of anything else to say to her.

I went back indoors to talk to Mum and Dad and

they told me everything, and all three of us cried a bit and they said they really wished they'd told me about the baby – my sister – before. Eventually, hours later, we all went to bed, but I couldn't sleep. I was thinking of all the things between Zara and me which couldn't be unsaid, and how everything was now all wrong and horrible. Had I been awful to her? Thoughtless? Patronising? If I'd been nicer, a better friend, would she have done what she had? If I hadn't snubbed her when I'd been with my brother? If I hadn't sneakily thought she was a bit of a pikey? If I hadn't wanted to be accepted by The Four so much? If . . . if . . . There were so many ifs, but I didn't think any of them added up to doing what she'd done – or had tried to do – to my family.

And After...

I was dreading seeing Zara at school the following week, but she didn't come back. She was absent for the rest of that term and then I heard that because her mum was still drinking and she'd got so much in debt, the landlord had chucked them out of their flat. They'd had to go and live with Zara's aunt in Wales.

I felt a bit sorry for her then, but not much. I never tried to get in touch with her or anything. Things had gone too bad between us for that.

At school, everything gradually got back to normal. Anton went back to France and by then Sophie wasn't even seeing him. Pretty soon – by the middle of the following term – she and Sky began speaking again, and there was a big reconciliation scene at school with them throwing their arms around each other and crying. India and Chloe became friends again too – I helped that by telling Chloe how Zara had found out about her brother. I explained to everyone about my mum and dad and the baby, too.

Of course, we talked about Zara pretty much non-stop for weeks and weeks, and I told them that at the start she and I had planned some of the tricks together, just for a laugh, but that what had happened afterwards I'd believed just as much as they had.

At Christmas Lois paid to go to a psychic gypsy woman who told her that inexperienced people should never try to contact the dead, and that doing stuff with a ouija board was just asking for trouble. She didn't get any message from her mum, anyway, even from the real deal. And I never again saw the boy I called Lofty, so all the things Zara said about him and me having a future were just a load of rubbish.

Things at school are pretty good again now. I go round with Poppy most of the time because Lois's dad got a contract in Germany and they've gone to live there for a year, and Poppy and I have quite a laugh. I do think about Zara sometimes – but not often. And if no one shouts goodbye when I get off the school bus I try not to mind too much . . .

Mary Hooper

Mary Hooper has been writing professionally for over twenty years. Her first experience of writing success was in the magazine world; she had hundreds of short stories and serials published in teenage and women's titles. After this she was inspired to begin writing books, and so wrote a stream of humorous and realistic teenage novels, plus a batch for younger readers.

In the last few years Mary has achieved many plaudits for her challenging series of *Megan* titles about a fifteen-year-old girl who has a baby. She won the 2001 North East Book Award for the first book in this series. Mary has also written two historical novels: *At the Sign of the Sugared Plum*, and *Petals in the Ashes*.

Mary describes her hobbies as 'pottering, doing things with dried flowers, painting furniture, moving pictures around on walls and collecting china rabbits'. She lives in an old cottage in Hampshire where all her hobbies are indulged!

www.maryhooper.co.uk

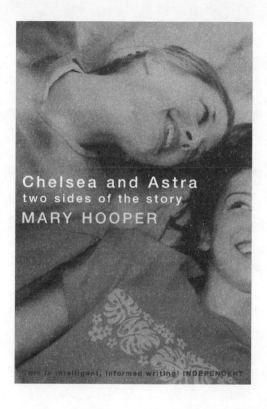

Chelsea and Astra
two sides of the story
MARY HOOPER

'This is intelligent, informed writing' INDEPENDENT

BLOOMSBURY

www.bloomsbury.com

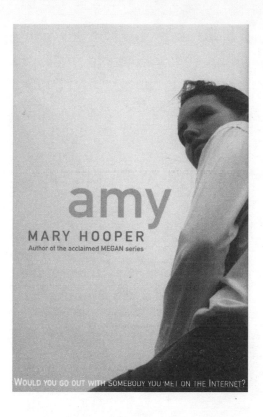